MINDFUL THINGS

TALES FROM A TILTED WORLD

Tara Lee Davis

For

My grandfather Tony "Da" Fortes

Who laid the tracks
one smile at a time.

You are missed.

~*~

My husband Jason
and my minions Alyssa and Scott

You are my present
and my future.

I love you.

ACKNOWLEDGMENTS

Thank you to my wonderful husband Jason for whispering sweet things, making me laugh every day, and ensuring I don't spend too much time in my *noplace*. I heart you.

For Alyssa and Scott, I am proud of you both. Thank you for hugging and loving me at my best and even when you awaken the Mommy Troll in the morning. All of me loves all of you.

Thank you for all my family (New Bedford/Fairhaven forever!) and my mother-in-law who love me, accept me as is, and for all they do.

A special note of appreciation to my early beta readers Amy Bee, Danielle Dayney, Gail Webber, Trond Hildahl, and Ana Pascoe who helped me in the monumental task of supporting me during the polishing of my first manuscript.

Thank you to my cousin, Tracey, for connecting me with her photographer friend Tara-Marie who generously allowed the inspiring photograph of Tracey to be used as my first book cover.

This book would not have been possible without the continued support of my writing collective, virtual community friends and peers from YeahWrite.me, ScribesUnite, and the WriteNow crew from NYCM. You all helped me find my inner writer again.

TABLE OF CONTENTS

CHAPTER ONE
Mindful Things

AT DAWN, THE INTERCOM CHIMED and widened its oculus. A serene, feminine computer voice murmured, *"Bonan matenon,* Dr. Landry. Be mindful; be aware; be at peace, for you are not alone."

Already awake, she waited for the sun to throw orange beams through the wide, bare window. Above it, a hand painted slogan echoed the morning's standard greeting: *Observi, Konscii, Paca.* The floor bed dominated the spartan space, a single ceiling light cast a dim glow, and the heated floor provided a welcome creature comfort. In this place, routine, mindfulness, and focus guided actions. Roll the mattress, fold the bedding, and place them in the lower closet. Store the pajamas in the upper compartment and exchange them for the forest-green day attire. Predictable, simple, and uncomplicated.

So. Damn. Tranquil.

Brief, sweet solitude beckoned from the toilet closet. Technology was forbidden to residents and unauthorized staff, but information didn't need wires to travel. A quick search produced a blue wooden disk from behind the tank and she slipped it under the waistband of her pants. A summons. She palmed a sleek Ruger .380 lady's pistol hidden beneath a corner floor tile. It was too small for most men's meaty fingers to fire, but it packed a full-sized kick. The specially made

1

ankle holster did not bulge under the required uniform. The weapon reminded her not to get lost in serenity.

In the separate washroom, she reached for the toothbrush with her right hand, hesitated, and turned on the dual faucet instead. The mirror reflected the crow's feet around her eyes and the wall camera behind her. *Never alone,* she reminded herself. She splashed water on her face, smoothed her brown hair back with wet fingers, and remembered to grab the toothbrush with her left.

Life stirred in the *L'arbaro Retreto Kunsido* facility—The Forest Retreat. Many bare feet padded to the rhythm of wordless greetings. People assembled here for solace, inner contemplation, and protection—or surveillance, depending on the point of view. Though guests brought their mother language with them, solidarity sprang from the simple Esperanto lexicon. Familiar, friendly faces acknowledged her, and she identified each in a mental checklist.

Traffic moved to the lower levels for the daily walking meditation, but she broke away to follow the polished floor past the busy kitchen to the offices. Her stomach rumbled as her fingertips tapped the door, and it slid open. One worker skimmed by with a wide, soft push broom.

"*Sani*—be well. Enter, please, June." A woman, her face obscured by a hooded white and green robe, stepped aside to allow entry. The door closed with a soft *shiff*. The office contained only a desk with an outmoded internal landline, two comfortable chairs, and walls of books.

"*Sani, Profesoro* Gale."

The founder of the revitalized facility held aloft a silver tube and lasers swept the room high and then low. A green light indicated that it detected no listening devices in their immediate area. The woman put a finger to her hidden lips to caution, though the motion resembled a polite greeting with her palms pressed together.

"I hope your stay here has met all your expectations."

June returned the gesture. "It has, but I am eager to get back to other projects."

"I understand. Six months is a long time. Solitude can be a burden. Your help in aiding me with personal and professional matters has been invaluable. I ... please consider any obligation you feel paid in full."

"I'm sure my replacement will be more than adequate."

"As you pointed out—younger than ideal and an inch too short. But, she'll do. I trust your judgment."

Profesoro Gale Melody peeked out the frosty window and studied the workers clearing pathways. "The project is secure for now. It's been—quiet."

"That may change when we leave the campus next week. The security here is exemplary, but out there—"

"—there's a price on what Dr. June Landry knows."

"Can't stay here forever."

"*Observi, konscii, preta,*" the *Profesoro* faced June and whispered the last word, but her lip movements were clear. Be mindful, be aware, *be ready.*

∞

Heavy snowfall in the night had transformed three hundred acres of pristine central Massachusetts woodlands into a snow oasis. June shrugged in the provided parka, ski pants, and heavy snow boots. The outside air crisped the breath and stung the cheeks. Blinding sunlight bounced off the fresh powder. The grounds staff armed themselves with shovels and machines to clear hazards and assure that everyone could move around the facility safely. There might not be another opportunity in the next few days to see a crystal-clear view from the top of the hiking trail. No clouds marred the icy blue sky.

Meditation didn't end for another hour and she had the grounds to herself for the first time. At the equipment desk, she signed out binoculars with a built-in camera. June followed the slick, plowed routes using a ski pole for balance. Except for the extra work activity outdoors, nothing unusual garnered attention.

"*Bonan matenon,*" a man from behind a mini-plow greeted, his face ruddy.

"*Sani,*" June replied recalling his name, Rainer Sands.

"Early today?" He cupped a hand over his eyes against the brilliant snow shine. "The view is beautiful. Some of the trail's cut; watch the ice!"

"*Danko!*" She waved and continued along the cleared path.

The celebrity of her initial arrival had long settled. A week or two of, "Are you *the* Dr. June Landry? The neuroscientist?" followed by, "What's it like to win a Nobel Prize?" and the inevitable, "Is it true? Can you erase memories?"

The work proved itself first on animals. Dr. Landry developed a way to target the right synapses. The red tape for a single human subject took years—the ethics argued and debated by peers—the strict regulations outlined in a 150-page legal document. The widely publicized paper stated, "*The ME-MR protein successfully and permanently removed the subject's traumatic memory during an induced critical window.*"

TIME, *Science*, and the *New York Times* espoused the virtues of the discovery for victims of PTSD, Alzheimer's, and other crippling brain maladies. *A patient debilitated by post-traumatic stress could find relief,* dozens of newscasters reported. The other side of the argument, though, shone a spotlight on the darker aspects of ME-MR. Why not wipe a mind clean and insert a custom made one? Erase your enemies. Create true political puppets.

An attack on the Landry lab mainframe proved that the threats and conspiracy theories had teeth. Two attempted kidnappings, multiple hacks, and laboratory moles forced drastic measures: isolation, secrecy, and paranoid tactics. ME-MR had not been stored on any system accessible to cyber-terrorists. Only one person had access to all proprietary information.

June gasped from the effort of the climb to the observation platform. Half of it still lay under snow. Her exhalations became visible white speech balloons. The echoing roar of snow throwers disturbed the quiet, but the sounds were a welcome change. She scanned the landscape through the binoculars. Security towers blended into the landscape and she photographed the men below digging out the drifts. Lights indicated that electricity or generators functioned. Rainer's mini-plow approached, the engine huffed, and idled. A shovel scraped and scuffed. Satisfied with the start of the daily rounds, June stepped away, turned, and smiled at Rainer. He didn't smile back. His fist connected with her jaw with a precise force that snapped her head to the side. Her body crumpled, and her face smacked the deck.

∞

Rainer roused her with slush down her shirt and a few taps to the cheek. June's black eye and swollen cheek obscured her vision on one side; her lip bled and dripped down her chin. Zip ties bound her wrists and ankles. The sun, just past peak, cast dappled light and deep shadows on the forest floor. Her assailant propped her body up against a pine. His short black hair dripped with sweat and his face flushed with adrenaline.

"Goddamn! I thought you'd never leave the fucking herd."

June grasped for consciousness. Another slap stung. "I'm awake dammit!" She raised bound hands to block the blows.

"Good."

They'd cleared the file on Rainer. He'd checked out and was on payroll over a year. Helpful, punctual, and a hard worker. Perhaps a little free with the ladies and liquor, but nothing out of the ordinary for a divorced man his age. He'd played the long game. An agency or a man for hire?

"Where's the lab? I know it's here."

"I don't kn—"

He silenced her with a booted kick.

"Don't test me."

June grunted and pulled her knees to her chest, assessing the situation while feigning submission. The interrogation in the middle of the woods and the sweat he wiped from his upper lip betrayed his agitation. June surmised he'd seized a desperate opportunity and abandoned plans. Rigid routines, monitored cameras, and the safety of numbers had been his undoing.

Got deadline, asshole? A free agent with no handler to direct or bail you out, maybe?

"Can't find it on your own? All that time wasted," she taunted, squinting with her good eye.

He clenched her throat with powerful fingers and squeezed until her windpipe burned. When she began to lose consciousness, he let go. She strained to suck in sweet, icy air. "Careful," she wheezed. "Damage the merchandise too much and you won't get paid." The snow turned pink where she spat blood.

His fingers curled in her hair and yanked until her eyes teared. He ground her sore face into the tree. The smell of the snowmobile gasoline on his hands prickled her nose.

"The lab."

"I told you I don't—"

He pressed a knee down on both her legs, grinding muscle against bone until she howled. "You'll give me what I want."

Rainer tapped her fingers, counted them, then kissed the ring finger. Her heart raced, and rapid breaths chapped her parted lips. A pair of pliers *snipped* in front of her nose. Snap. Snap. Snap. When she struggled to curl her fingers, he pressed between a knuckle to straighten them. The pliers' teeth grabbed her fingernail and Rainer yanked. He made her look at him when he muffled her screams with his hand. Her agonized shrieks grew hoarse, she vomited through his fingers, and he pressed the back of her head into the bark harder.

"One," he rasped in her cold-burned ear. "Where?" Snap. Snap.

She squeaked, "I don't know!"

When her screams died he targeted the next digit. She begged and kicked, desperate under his weight. He kissed her temple and sucked her index finger until it warmed. Rainer savored the time—wiping her welling tears away. He curled his lip, denuded the nail bed, and forced back the renewed screams with his palm.

"Shhh." He kissed the back of her hand. "Which one next?" Snap.

When she came to, shock tremors shook her, and weakness slackened her muscles. Salty, frozen snot hung from her nostrils. The numbing cold was a welcome relief to her four mangled left fingers. Rainer, his back turned, pissed on a nearby tree. Through one eye, she watched the warm vapors rise around him. Fresh snow absorbed and muffled sound.

June tightened the zip tie around her prominent wrist bones with her teeth until it impaired circulation. Raising her arms above her head, she brought her hands down hard, aiming her elbows past her ribcage close to her hips. Rapid motion produced torque and the plastic snapped. The sting and gouges hardly registered.

The Ruger found a steady grip in her uninjured, dominant hand. Slumping to one side to mislead Rainer and conceal the weapon behind her leg, she let him saunter back. He'd left his button undone and belt hanging. The metal *tinged* with each step.

"Dr. Landry, you're a tough old bitch." He sneered close, his hot breath crawling up her nose.

She snorted with derision and raised the pistol. "I'm not Dr. Landry." The amusement died on Rainer's face seconds before the bullet ruined it.

∞

In the hidden safe-room at the rear of the office, the *Profesoro* shed her hood and administered first aid. "If you won't let me call the facility medic, at least let me get someone at the lab to attend to you."

"I'll live. Call the number I gave you. They'll take care of the body. No one knows the truth. We need to do everything we can to keep it that way."

"This man, Rainer, had no idea?"

"No," She lifted her bandaged left hand to emphasize that she wasn't a natural southpaw. "I don't think he had any vested interest other than money, either. If he couldn't get answers, he was willing to kill me—or, rather, you."

The *Profesoro*, the real Dr. Landry, frowned. "I feel responsible, Dana."

Dana hugged her throbbing hand to her chest and shook her head. "Don't. I fucked up."

The women, though not identical, shared a close enough resemblance. Dr. Landry's nose had been broken in a minor car accident and matched sufficiently with Dana's brawl hardened one. Advancing age obscured other facial features sufficiently. Anyone that only knew the doctor by brief acquaintance or through pictures wouldn't notice the switch.

"Maybe money had nothing to do with it. Maybe he was supposed to kill the research." Dr. Landry's voice wavered.

"Possible." Dana sucked in her breath when a wet cloth rasped the facial scrapes. "Your work is important. What you did for me…for my family…I can't forget that."

"You've done enough."

"I'm not close to done yet. I'm going to find the sons-of-bitches who hired that prick." Dana clenched a fist and tightened her face into a scowl. "Is my replacement ready?"

Dr. Landry nodded while applying liquid stitches to Dana's minor facial wounds. "She took to the new procedure well. The memories are placed; reinforcement will strengthen them. As you said when you selected her, she's—eager."

"Good. I suggest you don't leave the facility, yet. We'll make the decoy exchange here instead." Dana winced and swallowed four painkillers. "I think Dr. Landry should decide to take up deep meditation and solitude for a while until the current guests have gone, yes?"

In their time working together, the doctor persona had become abstract—a suit to put on. Trading places had become as mundane as changing shoes.

"And you?"

"Oh, I'll get back to what I do best." Dana's cheeks warmed with excitement. "Someone knows something. You don't find a guy like that without having to go through a few people."

Dr. Landry removed her robes with shaky hands, hesitated, and handed them to her decoy and bodyguard.

Dana slipped into the guise of *Profesoro* Gale Melody and the fabric swallowed her.

∞

Feeling naked without the anonymity of a hood, Dr. Landry waited until the hall emptied for evening meditation. Slender privacy blinds in the outer office let in slivers of the last of the evening light. Dana put a comforting, undamaged hand on her shoulder. The silence crushed; the cameras watched.

The doctor brushed her left fingers along the textured wall, bypassed the kitchen, and scurried up the stairs. She found no reassurances in the empty sleeping chamber as she prepared for the long night. For a few days it would sound strange when people called her June. She would remind herself that she wasn't the *Profesoro* anymore and return a silent nod. Her research in the satellite lab beneath the complex would wait. In the meantime, she'd work the problems in her head and continue the plan for moving to the new location with her new replacement decoy in place.

The intercom chimed.

"*Bonan nokton*, Dr. Landry. Be mindful; be aware; be at peace, for you are not alone."

Tara Lee Davis

CHAPTER TWO

Night Run

BLOOD DRIPPED FROM THE TWO-pronged faucet wrench in Sonja Desenna's right hand, and the slender man dropped to his knees holding his neck.

The delivery van's front had crumpled like a tin can when the truck swerved, almost pushing it over into the Monroe City Reservoir. The engines idled. Gravel dust floated in the beam from the truck's headlights.

He's got five minutes before he bleeds out.

She struggled to catch her breath. Her palms and face burned from their scuffle on the ground. She could still feel his fingers crushing her throat.

Glass littered the ground and gas hissed from a keg rolling into the middle of the road. The smell of cheap beer mixed with the heady scent of wild honeysuckle. The van's blinkers clicked on and off. The dying man gurgled, sputtered, and his shoes scraped on the road. He sunk shoulder first to the ground.

She was alone.

Sonja dropped the improvised weapon and struggled to loosen the false bottom on one of the damaged kegs where Jan had stored the backup firearms. It refused to budge.

Shit!

11

Her own gun and knife had been lost to the dark slopes during the fight. Sonja limped to retrieve a slender, silver canister rolling amid debris then flung the dead man's pistol and taser into the tree line. The ident-locks rendered them useless to her. Metal clanged against metal when Sonja tried to loosen the false bottom with the canister.

How did they find us? New protocol maybe? Squealer?

Her partner, Jan, had brawled with the assailant and both had tipped over the side of the low road wall. They'd tumbled down the steep grassy incline to the water below. The grunts and heavy footfalls scrambling back up weren't Jan's.

Sonja abandoned her search for a weapon and scurried to the forested embankment on the opposite side of the road. She held her tender left arm close to her body and pressed her other hand against her side to relieve the pain. Four old towns had been flooded to create the massive water reserve, and the expanse was too far to swim even without a broken toe, yanked ankle, and bruised ribs.

The woods swallowed her.

The moist embankment was lit only by the quarter moon and each slipped step tumbled her into a trunk or thorny brush. Snapping shrapnel from a silent shot, burst a few feet away and peppered her face. Cursing followed several dud trigger clicks. Her pursuer, even weighed down by wet clothing and slowed by the darkness, crashed through branches and brush at a pace that Sonja couldn't match.

When footfalls faltered, his body thumped about five-hundred feet away. Sonja veered left, slid several feet, picked a careful horizontal path, and waited behind an old growth oak. Her pursuer, a vague outline in the dark, bulldozed through, swearing at his weapon.

The breeze tickled the water and cooled the sweat soaking down her neck and back. Blood poured from the gash in her scalp. She gagged at the metallic taste and saliva felt like a lead ball in her throat. When a yelp from some distance followed a crunch and splash, she held her ribs while following the white and orange glow back up to the road. Bark and thorns tore her palm as she fumbled for hand grips to pull herself up, using the canister as a piton.

∞

The truck whined, groaned, and sputtered out. The sound reverberated across the reservoir. She tightened her sore hands around the canister and leaned her throbbing forehead to the steering wheel for a second.

He heard that. After that fall, he's got to be hurt. If I had a gun I could stop at the old church and pick him off.

Her numbed foot swelled even though she'd only been sitting for a couple of minutes. If she made it to within weapons range of the checkpoint she might shake him off that way. With a shot from the emergency kit in the glove box to further dull the pain, she could run the bridge on foot and take a shortcut through the utility road. She fumbled with the palm-sized kit in the glove box, dialed the med injector, and shot the painkiller into her leg. Sonja wrinkled her nose against the scent of fuel and hot brakes and stumbled out of the vehicle. Branches snapped.

She ran.

At first, she dragged her mangled foot, but as the medicine separated her from the jarring strikes and burning breaths, she managed to pick up decent speed. A count in her mind focused and motivated her to go just a little further. If she could run to ten once, she could run to ten again.

Before she reached the end of the access bridge, he'd caught up and was dogging her heels although he was limping and wheezing. Sweat blurred her vision. His proximity curled the hairs at the nape of her neck and the reach of his fingers brushed her shirt. The shortcut aside the road turned sharp right and dipped suddenly. She dropped, rolled, and skidded, kicking up dust in the dark.

"Bitch!" he yelled, tripping and thudding hard over something.

∞

The stone church marked the halfway point. Sonja vaulted the cobbled walls hoping the black landing points weren't potholes or debris. Her legs buckled. A knee slammed into a rock, sending throbs down her leg. She righted herself and pushed forward, skirting around the faint outlines of broken columns. The man grunted, fruitlessly triggering his jammed weapon, and slammed into a crumbling archway. Debris tumbled.

Sonja gasped. Every breath inflated her lungs to bursting, but it wasn't enough. Soon he had closed the space between them again. She exhaled crushed and empty.

Not yet. Not yet. A little further.

She tightened her grip on the canister, wheeled around, and cracked the man in the face with it.

The momentum sent them both to the ground, though Sonja was first up and able to build up a distance. From behind he panted and swore, narrowing the gap just as the subtle outline of the checkpoint appeared at the top of the final incline.

When fingers brushed her shirt again she flung the canister at his head. It clanged against a rock. The man's shoes ground into the loose stones when he charged after it.

"Alice finds the rabbit!" Sonja shouted with one arm in the air. She knew lookouts had her in their sights, ready to pull triggers the moment she was in range. A scout would be nearby somewhere, relaying the words she kept rasping. She hoped.

An old engine sputtered and the gates opened enough to allow one person through at a time. Shouts followed warning shots. Sonja struggled over the blockade of cars, jeeps, and barrels, quick hands helping to haul her over a hood by her belt loops. She collapsed after closing the distance to the gate.

∞

Dr. Loring peered over her glasses and pressed the dozen, elongated, inch-long bumps under Sonja's left arm. The doctor sucked her tongue.

"One's broken. The synth-tag is in your system now. You can't go back again for at least a year," she said, beginning to extract the tubules one by one from the tender flesh. "You'll be fine otherwise."

"Doesn't matter. Jan didn't make it." Sonja's dry eyes stared into nothing.

She thought of Jan and her recruitment four years ago when the plague had just begun to claim the poorest. Sonja had played the part of the oblivious data grunt at work but had been forging med records for three years. Fake documents could be slid one or two at a time into a batch group under a company employee name one or more times (including her own to ensure the illusion of randomness).

Although never greedy and staunchly cautious about who she helped, Sonja had erred. Jan, a coworker from another division, had warned her and misdirected the authorities. Data decoys and paper trail red herrings had kept her from discovery.

Dr. Loring did not look up from her work until the last had been extracted. "This will help cure a lot of people."

The doctor sent an assistant off with the merchandise to begin the slow replication process and stood for a moment in front of a creaky fan. "You're the only one who made it so far. Let me see your foot. Broken is it? You said you ran the whole way?" Muted, muttered conversations carried through the open door before it closed again. "The scouts said whoever it was had you dead to rights."

Sonja stared at the stained drop ceiling and counted the holes in the tiles. "He wanted that canister more than me. The cargo was all he cared about."

It had been nothing more than a metal tube filled with dead fruit flies. He'd made the wrong choice, she'd been carrying the sought-after DNA fragments in her body. They coded for a treatment for the plague afflicting the exiled populace who couldn't afford the cost— people she couldn't have helped through forged documents alone.

"Clever putting it in yourself."

"Jan's idea. Said back-ups weren't enough—it was always better to have a decoy."

CHAPTER THREE

Choices

STEAM HIT MY FACE AND poured from the antique microwave moments before an egg boiling in the mug exploded with the bang of a cherry bomb. The pressure flung the door open, almost bruising my nose. I clutched my chest and righted my fogged glasses that had been knocked askew. Kevin cracked up until tears ran and he slipped off the kitchen stool. I never thought to hear that sound from the skinny ten-year-old who'd begged me not to call authorities when I found him three days ago locked in the cellar. He needn't have grabbed my leg and put a run in my stocking, the old phones hadn't worked in decades. I hadn't even brought my mobile-com since tech outside of the cities had long since stagnated.

"Child, you can't be boiling an egg like that!" I handed him a wet cloth and steered him toward the mess. "We put right what went wrong."

I left to shower off the red dirt that clung to creases I forgot I had. The stains never came out of the dungarees even after a good soak; they were more clay than denim. As I made braids of my grays, I thought about the hole I'd dug in the east field where the grass was ready for scything. I'd laid in it, wondering for an hour if it was more fitting to face up or down. It became clear that upward was for the peaceful who went in their sleep, curled on the side for ones that needed comfort or weren't ready, and down for the shame of a life lived at the expense of others.

Kevin's gentle knock coaxed me from my head. "Miss Vee, you okay?" He hesitated. "He'll be home soon."

He was quivering when I opened the door. I offered my hand in comfort and he collapsed into my chest, taking long inhales of my clean clothes. I found my own solace in his raspberry scented hair. It had taken three baths to clean him, four bowls to fill him, and many tissues to sort him out.

"Come sit. We got ourselves a decision to chew."

In the center of the vintage kitchen table, I placed my grandfather's pristine, heirloom Smith & Wesson .44 revolver. It had been a long time since I'd handled a firearm without a fingerprint ident-lock. "My grandpa wasn't happy when I enlisted. Left me all his guns though, 'cause he knew I understood."

Kevin had plopped himself in a rickety chair, pulled his knees up to his chest, and looked hard at me. The revolver's bright blue finish and walnut handle were unmarred except for a nick at the base.

"That's not a gun. That's a choice." I said, cleaning the smudges and lint from my lenses.

"With the war going on, ain't nobody going to care what happens out here, except us who's living it. This thing was done to you. The choice is yours."

He stared at the barrel and then flicked the unloaded piece with his finger to watch it spin on the white laminate table. I stayed his hand when he made to pick it up.

"No doubt it needs doing, but it ain't just on your shoulders. I've been on both sides of the trigger, you understand?" I rolled the bullets in my hand.

The refrigerator hummed.

"Do you still love your son?"

I pressed m lips together and rubbed the knot between my eyes. "I love the child I thought he was, not the man he is."

Kevin slid the gun towards me and I let out the breath I'd been holding. He'd be alright. There was still boy left in him yet.

"I'd've done it," he said, plucking at a string on the oversized shirt.

"Sometimes it's harder not to, isn't it?"

"You gonna send me away?"

He'd told me his family were all gone. They'd died soon after those high-hill schmucks decided to play chicken with The Button and dragged the world into another right mess. "It's worse in the boarding homes than ever, now," he'd told me. "I'd rather die here." I couldn't argue with the state of lawlessness the outer cities were in. Orphans outnumbered the adults and the age of emancipation had been lowered to fourteen just to get them out of one system and into another.

"I promised I wouldn't." I pointed. We could see the vehicle dust cloud from the window. "Hide where I told you. Don't come out 'til I call."

Sam arrived with a swagger that made me want to break his nose with my cast iron skillet. Had that contempt always wrinkled his nose? When had the first lie deceived me?

"Why the hell aren't you at the old folk's home?" His voice rose an octave and his eyes darted left like a deer facing the inevitable fender.

Old folk's home? I ought to have punched him just for that. "Move to the inner city," he'd urged me. A retirement community wasn't far from his overpriced, high-rise apartment. He'd sold me on the ME-MR integration VR therapy with the latest tech for PTSD treatment they offered for vets. Few seniors hadn't served at least two tours. "It could help, you know," he'd insisted.

Now, he ranted until I fired a warning shot that grazed his ear and busted my rooster cookie jar. I'd never wanted to leave my home, or the land generations of our family had toiled. The fractured company of my fellow veterans didn't compare to the familiar creature comforts of the ratty chair on the porch or the hand sewn quilt on the creaky four poster bed.

"I found the boy, Sam." I walked him to the hole that had taken two days to finish—fueled by my ire, contempt, and guilt. "How many have you broken and butchered? Do you even know?"

Had our fields harbored the dead? My mind wandered to the times when he'd come home as a young man in the summers and given a toy to his baby sister before returning to college—toys she'd been too young for. I'd found it endearing, and now the memories reeked with the taint of realizing they were trophies.

"Just strays. Nobodies. None that would be missed." He sniveled, and I made him look at me. "Mom, I swear, I'll stop."

"You will." My hand was a rock, but I trembled inside. "I got to put right what went wrong."

I made sure he was face down.

CHAPTER FOUR

A Rock and a Hard Place

THE FACE OF THE MOUNTAIN loomed.

"Your heart rate is elevated." The hovering gray orb zipped beside Vera's ear, buzzing and analyzing.

"Yes, Rex, it's called excitement." Vera placed her palms to the ground and ran her hands through the dirt.

"The substrate you are touching contains elevated levels of contam—

"Rex, initiate protocol 3104558."

"Are you sure? Alteration of protocol voids all—"

"Just do it, dammit!"

"Initiated."

The crickets and chirrup of birds soothed while the orb went about its business, quietly observing and waiting for input or an emergency. Vera shuffled through the tall grass and instructed Rex to display the map and satellite images. She picked her way to a flat area and after a few moments found the prize. The old, faded metal sign, half buried, still showed its two hundred and fifty-year-old letters: CAMP 4.

Rex clicked pictures and Vera placed the sign under the protection of a rock with respect. It had taken a week by hover-scooter to trek across the wilds, past the security barrier, to the place where humans once eschewed civilization to conquer and climb El Cap.

There hadn't been a human soul in Yosemite since the Nature Preservation Act when the environmental crisis had reached critical levels and powerful storms raged across the planet. Ground level cities had been retired long ago and humans shifted their living spaces to skyloft buildings and grew their food in hydroponic greenhouses. Terra firma was off limits for an indefinite period. Decades-old security protocols had grown lax, and Rex had bypassed the checkpoints with minimal effort.

Vera gazed up from the base of The Nose, the famous ascent Lynn Hill mastered in twenty-four hours in 1994, a record that was broken a decade later by Tommy Caldwell. She rested her hand on the warm rock and shivered. She'd done epic climbs indoors on progressively more complicated simulated runs since her early teens, but never had she touched an imperfect natural formation.

With a chute on her back, chalk bag, water, and food cubes, Vera prepared for a free climb. She hoped to find the marks of predecessors in the form of pitons or perhaps an artifact stuck in a crevasse. Rex's light turned red as Vera chalked her hands and began the ascent, but the new protocol prevented interference unless she fell.

Six hours in and puffing under the strain, Vera braced a foot on a ledge and leaned for a rest. Rex's primary function, like all obligatory monitors was her safety and it spun on its axis frantic to get Vera's attention.

"What is it, Killjoy." She sighed when the bot didn't respond and made a note to make further adjustments to the code. "Report, Rex."

"Your current vital levels are affecting performance. Music therapy has shown to improve focus. Might I play a selection?"

"That's the best idea you've ever had. Proceed."

The eerie trill of wind flapping around the rock face was drowned out by the sounds of Tom Petty's *Free Falling*.

"Very funny. Don't make me get my hammer."

"Humor has proven to relieve tension. Program 3104558 allows for adaptation to the given situation. You have only yourself to blame."

Vera pressed her forehead to the stone. "Find something inspiring in the archives appropriate for the occasion."

"File found in Victor's private collection. Shall I play it?"

She swallowed and bit her lip at the thought of her brother. "Proceed."

Vera resumed the climb concentrating only on the placement of finger and toe, inhale and exhale. Her foot slipped on a precarious nub and her body slid as she dangled from one hand wedged into a crack. Blood dripped from her chin, marking the stone. While she hugged the rock face and waited for the adrenaline shakes to pass, Vera reminded herself that she was fit and experienced with nothing to lose. Rex blared AC/DC's *For Those Who Are About to Rock We Salute You* throughout the valley.

Victor had always wanted to make this journey. "It's been a good, safe life of unextraordinary," he'd said. "Just once, I don't want to know what's coming. You know…make mistakes."

She refused to help him at first, fearing he'd be arrested and exiled to the cryochambers to sleep in peace until expiration. When he'd manifested a genetic cartilage hardening disease in his late twenties, his plans slipped and his spirit with them. Official *medreps* assured her that the mutation was a spontaneous anomaly, and their family's genetic lineage remained secure—as if that information made all the difference.

The last months were not happy ones, but the medics made him as comfortable as possible. Vera had spent two years coding a special VR simulation for Victor's end of life protocol. In his delirium, he thought he had climbed The Nose and found his bliss.

"You should see this. It's perfect," were his final words.

Vera wondered if he'd known it was a beautiful lie. When the last foot of three thousand was in her grasp, Vera hauled her spent body over the top and lay immobile. "Rex, time."

"Twenty-five hours, twenty-eight minutes, seven seconds."

"Not bad for my age."

"At thirty-nine—"

"Shut up, Rex. Let me have my moment."

Vera rubbed her wind-rasped face and stretched weary, aching fingers. She'd gone through a lot of tape and the blisters flamed.

"Rex, create a sim of Victor. Postulate what he'd do and say." She'd provided Rex with every recording, photo, and piece of data that ever existed for Victor. Vera had reprogrammed the bot to be his echo; she had a way with code and didn't much care for the drudgery of sanctioned programs required of her job.

"Projecting."

The image smiled at her, lifted its arms, and whooped. "Amazing! And you said we couldn't do it!"

"Wrong. I said you were a selfish asshole and were crazy wanting to drag me into it." Vera wiped her nose on the hem of her shirt. "Now, I'm a felon."

The ethereal Victor winked. "Only if you get caught."

The projection took several giant steps back. "Fastest way down is to fly," it said, laughing and leapt off the summit with an echoing *whoo hoo.*

"That was perfect, Rex. He was always a bad influence."

Vera stood, closed her eyes, and jumped. The updraft churned her hair and stung her face. Her hollers were decidedly less enthusiastic than the sim's.

Rex deployed the chute at a precise determined moment, but not before falsely reporting to Vera that the initiation sequence had experienced a malfunction.

CHAPTER FIVE

Palindrome

I DIED ON SEPTEMBER SECOND in the year 2090 and was born on September twenty-first in the year 2129. As the saying goes, I wasn't *all dead*. A bad reaction to medication caused a super-cerebromedullospinal disconnection—a malfunction between mind and body. A person retains all consciousness and higher function, but can't move at all, except for their eyes. Ninety-percent die within four months. My case was "super" because I didn't have even eye movement nor the luxury of death. Instead, I dreamed. A machine told them I existed—locked inside myself. I caused quite the sensation! They thought about calling my unique and puzzling condition Sleeping Beauty Syndrome, but that was taken. Instead, they settled on Caer's Syndrome.

I know these things because of my personal nurse, Blair who spoke to me even if she thought I couldn't hear. I didn't realize for some time that I experienced acute lag-time and couldn't understand things as they occurred, but only when they passed. It wasn't unlike gazing at starlight only to discover that the visible twinkling originated from a star long dead. What a mind fuck that is. Yet, my mind is peculiar, and I found ways around it.

I always imagined Blair with black hair dyed in a rainbow of bright colors, held aloft in two pony tails so that she could wear her nurse's hat at a saucy angle. In my inner eyes, her face always changed, but she wore the traditional white dress and shoes with ridiculous socks. It must have been her berry-scented grooming products that made me hallucinate her that way. What a comfort her voice was.

Sometimes she held cotton balls under my nose that smelled of wonderful things like chocolates, apple pie, and roast turkey. She would tell me when she turned on lights She described the room and detailed the outfit of the day. She relayed news, played music, and read my favorite books (plus a few torturous volumes). When they brought in the experimental full body suit dotted with electrodes to stimulate my muscles, Blair told me it was a hideous display of blue polka dots on a white and black chevron pattern. Once, she brought her daughter, June, and I delighted in her cherry smell and skipping giggles. A million whats and ten thousand whys poured from her.

Most of the time a *nothing* took up space. It was different than losing myself in thought when time didn't pass at all. My husband used to put a hand on my shoulder, clasp my hand with his warm sausage-fingers and ask, "Where'd you go?" I'd smile and say, "No place." Sometimes I'd drift away in the middle of a movie and come back to credits yet feeling like only a moment had passed. Funny, I'd forgotten I'd had a husband. The aroma of lily-of-the valley would overtake me when he...used to visit.

Nothing wasn't like the *noplace*. This lag time went the other way. A forever of hours wasn't bliss. It was a suffocating gray that consumed memory and every sensation. My brain manifested an interpreter to reconcile the lag. I called her Connie. She would sit suspended in the nothingness until I asked, "What's on tonight, Connie?" Then I could know what had happened.

Blair's snippets were among the most vivid as she never seemed to stop talking. I visualized all that she described; I felt for brief moments that I was *out there*. Even if it was little more than a snapshot, I

longed for each lifeline. Then one day, Connie had no news from Blair anymore, and I didn't visit the news-void for a long time. I cannot say for how long, for time seemed at once short and infinite.

Most of my time I spent in dreams that grew increasingly bizarre and found it difficult to remain in a lucid state. The fear of getting lost prompted me to return to Connie who told me that the prognosis was poor, my closest living relatives had signed the order, and I'd been moved to the cryogenic program. No one thought to explain it to me like Blair. Perhaps my body lay in a dark box in a drawer upon a wall. Hundreds of technically-dead popsicles waiting to thaw in a living morgue.

Imagining myself in a glass tube wasn't my brightest idea. I would've been better off envisioning white beaches or powdery snowcaps. Faces or voices that I should have known thinned and disappeared in the *nothing*. In time I didn't know if I had a family or only imagined I had one. My own face eluded me. How could a person forget the color of their own eyes?

Threads holding the pieces of myself frayed. Terrified, I tried again to find an exit: mirrors, bed knobs, fireplaces, tunnels, manholes, keyholes, wardrobes, and old doors. None worked to connect me to the outside.

On a whim, I followed a recurring dream I had previously ignored. The dream version of myself labored hard in a farmhouse in the middle of the night. I didn't know our name and didn't think to ask. I touched the other me and my hand went through her belly, distorting like a dream mirror.

"Not yet," she panted, speaking through gritted teeth, "Soon! We've almost got it."

Well, damn. That pumped some life into me! I thought to ask myself if I was my own subconscious, but I got stuck trying to understand to the logic of my own question.

Despite the conundrum, I felt drawn to that dream at the exclusion of all others, looping it over and over. I stopped counting after 2012 because I feared each roll was a day in my life wasted.

I couldn't stay away. Something was better than *nothing*.

The dream blipped during one of its incarnations—a hiccup in the pixels. I placed my hand upon my alternate's abdomen. I fell in, crashed into an icy white pit, and opened my real eyes. I gasped.

The collective music of numerous voices threw me back harder than I expected. My lost anatomy began to re-materialize. Tremors followed fully-boy pins and needles. Pain!

"Can you hear me, Kaira? Feel that?"

My eyes wept incalculable yeses.

CHAPTER SIX
Comply

THE ELECTRONICS RAN HOT, AND the sharp ozone odor burned like pins and needles in Cera's nose. They'd given her something that prevented blinking and clear contacts protected her eyes. The paralyzing medication numbed the sensation of breathing and caused a peculiar perception of floating above the surface she lay upon. When they'd placed her naked body on it, she'd expected cold, unyielding metal. Instead, dense gray foam molded over her ears as her weight sunk. Each finger had its place and the soft mass plugged each ear.

Similar material lined the whole of the room in a muted gray. The wall corners muddled into nothing, disguising the room's size. A vast fog became a stone sarcophagus. Cera's rushing blood filled her head in a panic tide when the clear biofilm lowered from above to complete the encasement. She tried to look to the side, but her eyes stared up, immobile. The vacuum seal pressed against every hair until nothing quivered and there was only the gray.

An artifact moved slowly across her vision field and she imagined it a scream caught, contained, and crushed.

∞

In the control room, Cera's vitals—coded in colored lines and numbers—glowed silently on black screens. The head technician, Dr.

29

Bianca Bell, adjusted her slender headset and ordered the computer to initiate white noise and to hold for further instruction.

"How long is this going to take? Time is a waste of credits." Benton Jaqquer had enough wealth to afford him the luxury of not needing patience. A journalist once reported that a Jaqquer would tell Death that they didn't see anyone without an appointment.

Dr. Bell pushed her hands into the gray lab coat pockets and studied the data to be sure the subject was coping. "Depends. Do you want your imm broken or psychotic?"

Jaqquer glanced through the two-way mirror down at his newly acquired property. Considered a danger to public safety and not to be trusted without a handler, the law supported popular opinion that the *inmortale* (imms) had their uses when properly managed.

"This one's been a house pet. No protocols whatsoever! No chip, no training, no purpose. Can you imagine? I won't lose my reputation if this one goes rogue." Jaqquer waved a dismissive hand.

Dr. Bell snorted and tapped the display keyboard. "We'll start with a conservative time perception shift of twenty-four hours." The computer complied, and a yellow bar on-screen filled then blinked green. "Cera," The doctor began.

"That's it? Nothing happened."

"Not to you."

"You should use the new assigned designation."

Dr. Bell refused to look at Jaqquer and only typed in a notation. "The imm needs to respond to something familiar. We need cooperative acceptance of the contract or it won't work."

She noted a spike in vitals and areas of the brain showing isolation markers. Dr. Bell could read the imm's mind just by interpreting colored and active regions in the brain scans.

"Cera. Imagine yourself playing handball whenever you want to indicate 'no', and imagine yourself walking through your home when you want to indicate 'yes'. Do you understand?"

After a pause the brain scan lit up and the doctor noted that it was yes and assigned a tone to the pattern.

"Now, tell me 'no'." Another area lit up in a mass of color and given a new tone.

"Are you ready to answer questions?" Dr. Bell scanned the output.

∞

After a stinging, shifting static, and a flash of orange Cera floated in the gray quiet and longed for something to happen. The gray and the silence stretched into a tunnel of nothing. When she used to think of nothing she thought it might be the blackest black or the brightest white. Gray was infinite melancholy.

Hello? She thought. *I want to go home!*

How long she had been disembodied she couldn't discern, but she'd recited all the poems and stories she could remember. She practiced simple calculations.

My name is Cera. Two plus two is four. Water bears are immortal and so am I. I am a me. They fear us, but we are the ones afraid.

She told herself riddles waiting for the oblivion of sleep and the relief of dreams, but both abandoned her.

Two plus two is … is … Those are a lot of tree frogs out there.

One by one she counted them as they hopped in the gray until their peeping became electronic chimes. She knew they weren't there, but it was better than the nothing. Better the hallucination than emptiness.

And then a voice called her name and she thought of hitting a handball until her hand felt a red smack and she lingered in the thoughts of her home.

I don't want to answer questions. I want to go home! I didn't do anything!

Cera imagined hitting a red ball over and over and over. Each manifestation vanished into a fog and the frogs chimed, until a sharp electrtric zap reset everything.

No. Wait! Don't leave me!

∞

Dr. Bell lifted a brow at the computerized voice chanting a monotone no. "Interesting," She swiped open a small screen. "Run search, compare data to—"

Jaqquer encroached on the doctor's space and pointed to the activation controls. "What are you waiting for? Do it again."

"The brain pattern looks—"

"Do you know what that is?" Jaqquer pointed out of the observation window at the body below. "More credits than your family will ever see in a thousand lifetimes. I want it tamed and ready for training."

Dr. Bell glanced away, her jaw tight. "It's only been a few minutes. We should wait. It's a shock at first. She's not acclimated."

Jaqquer opened his palm device, the circular platinum disk glowed with blue light. A holoreport hovered between them. He smirked. "Know what this is?"

"My transfer request."

"Dated five years ago." He *tsked*, snapping his fingers in front of her nose. "I'm feeling generous. I can make it happen. You can go anywhere you want and I'll erase that little debt of yours. You reset my property and I'll reset your life."

Dr. Bell bit her lip.

"It's just an imm. They've got all the time in the world. How about you?"

"Fine. I want an official document of agreement." The doctor's resin palm device chirped.

"Already done. Make it a week this time."

"Too much. There's a considerable risk of irreparable mental instability which will be useless to you. As I said before, the chip coding requires acceptance of the contract by the subject. It will work better if—"

"I can take my funding elsewhere." Jaqquer grinned. "Do it."

"Fine."

Cera waited an eternity and an eternity again. Without external stimulation, her brain grasped for input. The fog became engulfed by auditory squibs, visual halos, and pulsing fractals. The ability to tremble or weep would have brought a modicum of peace within the nothing.

Surrender would grant relief.

Voluntary servitude would end the depravation.

When the voice hugged her senses Cera thought she would burst. She answered the questions—careful not to hesitate or lose focus.

"Do you accept the contract? Will you comply?"

Questions burned. Each syllable an acid.

Cera thought of home.

A cruel yes.

CHAPTER SEVEN

The Right Questions

A BALL BOUNCED.
As I went up the apple tree, rotten apples fell on me. Bake a cake, steal a pie. Did you ever tell a lie? Yes, I did, and many times. Oh, you, tea. Out goes she. Drown in the middle of the deep blue sea.

A tin can crashed and startled Owen out of a haze on the couch. His eyes refused to open more than a squint against a blinding light reflecting off everything and nothing. A wicked headache screamed of a blackout night with too much drink. The blue-screened TV, old like the ones shown in virtual museums, flashed channel three.

The little voice began to sing again, and another can met its fate.

I need a smoke, he thought, stumbling for the door and shouting. "Quiet!"

His voice didn't carry far but bounced around him as if he were still in the house. Bright light burned his eyes and the concrete cooled his feet. Clattering. Skipping feet. Owen searched but found nothing but impossibly green trees and pristine pavement. A piercing whine vibrated his eardrums and forced his eyes shut.

In the next clear moment, he stood ankle deep in a mirror-still lake holding a bundle in his arms.

"Alright, Mr. Johnson, let's get started." The man in a crisp, blue linen coat gestured to his associate in gray.

"Owen. Call me Owen."

The two men glanced at each other. Gray made a notation on a file tablet while Blue conducted the interview.

"Your name is Charles Owen Johnson isn't it?"

Owen blinked grit from his eyes and spoke with a groggy slur. "My mother never called me Charles. Charles is my father. Can I get a smoke?"

"There's no smoking in the building." Blue slid a photo paper across the metal table. "What do you see? Do you recognize this?"

Owen focused and saw a picture of smiling little girl missing a tooth. "I don't know. A kid. Where am I?"

Blue's expressionless face offered no explanations. "Do you recognize this…girl?"

"I think so. Should I? Is there someone else in here?" Owen whipped his head from side to side, rubbing his stubbled chin on his shoulder. "I really need a smoke."

"That's all for now—Owen."

∞

A ball bounced.

As I was walking down the lake, I met a little rattlesnake. I fed him so much apple cake, it made his snakey belly ache. "How many rattles can you shake?" said the owl to the snake. One, two, three; out goes you, but not me.

The blazing white light blinded less outside where the air was placid, and leaves shivered with impossible greens. A girl skipped to the rhyme then threw a ball at a tin can alley on a low concrete wall. Her shoe lights winked red. She grinned gap-toothed, bunny-hopped until her braids were airborne, and waved him over to play.

Owen staggered backward, struggling for air, and zigzagged back to the house, puking from vertigo. He saw nothing come out, though he tasted soured bile and felt it dribble from his mouth and nose. The door yawned away and lurched forward to swallow him into the house's belly.

The toppling racket of cans echoed. The television flickered on a blank channel seven and the house winked out.

Quiet lake water lapped at Owen's ears and pressed at his back. From the corner of his eye a bundle floated. He reached out…

∞

"Let's get started, Mr. Johnson." The man in a crisp, blue linen coat stood next to his associate in gray.

"Owen. Call me Owen. Charles is my father." He scratched his ragged, itchy beard on his shoulder and licked the sourness from his lips. "Do I know you? Who else is here? Where am I?"

Gray made a notation on a file tablet while Blue held the photo paper inches away. "Do you recognize her."

"I need a smoke?" Owen strained against the migraine.

"There's no smoking in the building." Blue pressed. "Do you recognize her?"

Pressing his lips against a wave of nausea, Owen shook his head and balled his hands. His fingernails left divots in his palms.

"Are you sure? Look again."

A *shuffing* faded in the background. Owen furrowed his brow. "I think so. She lives in the house. I think? I feel sick."

Blue made a notation and motioned to Gray. "That's all for now, Mr. Johnson."

"Owen…Mr. Johnson's my father."

∞

A ball bounced.

As I went up the crimson hill, I met a hawker with good will. He had jewels, he had rings, he had many shiny things. He had a cat with nine tails. He had a hammer but no nails. One, two, run and shout. One, two and you're out.

Owen's fuzzy vision focused slowly from the outside edges to a pinpoint center. In and out of view of the picture window, a head with pigtails bobbed. A tin can racket punctuated the nursery rhyme.

He ran his hand along the view screen, but the channel wouldn't change from thirty-eight. Had he called the cable company for service? The days blurred one to the next. When he closed his eyes to the black, the lake took him. Dread lived there.

The brown-haired girl appeared in an armchair that hadn't been there before. She thumped her feet rhythmically as if sitting still were an impossible task. Her eyes laughed. She had one bare foot, one ratty sneaker, and water dripped from her drenched clothes. Her mouth chattered, but no sound registered. The chair abruptly shrank to a pinprick and the black erased the house until the lake waters tickled Owen's ankles. Had he walked to the lake?

In his arms, he cradled the girl. She stared cold. His heart raced. A chill began to spread to his hands.

Owen dropped her.

∞

"...Let's get started, Mr. Johnson." The man in a crisp, blue linen coat stood next to his associate in gray.

Owen couldn't stop the body shakes and his white-knuckled grip on the chair did little to quell the hand tremors. "Owen, my—." He licked the whiskers tickling his dry lips. "Do I know you?"

Gray made a notation on a file tablet.

Blue presented the photo paper. "Do you recognize this?"

Owen nodded.

"Do you know who she is? What can you tell me?"

"Her name's Deidre. Right? Deidre. She's seven. Yes. Seven." Owen struggled to make his lips form the words and to clear the cobwebs. "Got an aspirin? My head..."

Gray recorded and Blue questioned. "Deidre, you said? Anything else you can tell me?"

"She—She lives in the house—my house—with me. My house? She's mine I think. Right?" Owen squeezed his eyes shut and began to hyperventilate. "Man, I really need something for this headache."

"That's all for now, Owen."

"No...wait..."

∞

A ball bounced.

One, two, three, four. I hear a knock at the door. Nohn says to John, "How much are your geese?" John says to Nohn, "Twenty cents a-piece." Nohn says to John, "That's too dear." John says to Nohn, "Get away from here!"

Channel fifty-six.

Owen ignored the blue glow, rolled off the couch, and teetered outside to join Deidre who had her toothless grin ready. She would speak to him, but the voice faded out unless she sung a rhyme. Every day in the bright morning under an aquamarine sky, he'd watch her play. When she smiled, he smiled. When she goofed around he laughed. Never did her feet stop moving or her energy wane. How many minutes had gone today? Ten? Ten thousand? A blur crept around Owen's peripheral vision.

Deidre vanished mid-skip in a blink.

There. Then not.

Owen's heart sank, and his knees wobbled. He ran beyond the rock wall where the cans stood steadfast. He sprinted to *The Beyond*— the place on the other side of the wall with rolling, crimson hills to nowhere. Panic waves washed over him when the black began to wrap itself around him. He ran into the lake. His hand clutched a scruffy shoe.

Owen screamed.

∞

Owen screamed.

"Calm down, Mr. Johnson." The man in a crisp, blue linen coat sat next to his associate in gray.

"You have to find her!"

"Find who?" Blue asked after speaking to Gray in low tones.

"Deidre! She's gone. I—I lost her." Hysterical, Owen rasped the words through a dry throat. He tried to struggle and stand from the chair, but restraints immobilized him.

"How do you think you lost her?"

"I–I don't know. Should I know? Is that why I'm here? Because I lost her? I didn't mean to lose her. I was watching, I swear!" Owen struggled against the restraints.

"I believe you. You watched her for a long time. Is that right?"

"Yes—yes, I did. I've been watching. She's—she's the only—"

"That will be all for now…"

"No! Don't put me back!"

∞

A ball bounced.

One-ery, two-ery, dickery, Dan. Whack-a-mole, crack-a-mole, dockery, Pam. Thievery, dandy, step-in-time. Humbledy, bumbledy, ninety-nine. Oh, you, tea, out. You must go out!

Channel ninety-nine.

Silence.

Owen stumbled through the doorway. But the out was empty. The unrolling red ball was the brightest spot on the pavement. When he hopped the wall to search for Deidre, the lake met him in an instant. He fell forward and brawled with the still waters until it frothed and foamed. The lake morphed into a man's form and Owen attacked with fury.

"Give her to me!"

The inky lake writhed under his grip.

Deidre grasped his hands, but the liquid began to peel her away from his fingers. She had her mouth opened to laugh, but black froth bubbled from her lips and nose. Her eyes stared and turned an opaque blue. A piercing whine cut through his nerves and he squeezed harder. He lost one of Deidre's hands. Owen clawed and punched the waters, feeling it give under the force.

A banded weight crushed his chest and Deidre's other hand slipped. Owen pinched her fingertips tighter and dug his heels into the mud…

∞

"Alright, let's get started, Mr. Johnson." The man in a disheveled, blue linen coat sat next to his associate in gray whose hair was damp with sweat.

Owen breathed heavily and struggled in the chair against the restraints crushing his chest and numbing his limbs. "Put me back! I almost had her!"

"Back where, Mr. Johnson?"

"Back there. The house, the lake. I can save her. Put me back!" He wept and wanted to tear at his beard, but the restraints dug into his wrists. "She's at the lake."

"Do you feel responsible for her?"

Owen sobbed. "I almost had her..."

Gray and Blue glanced at each other, shook hands, and recorded new notes.

"Send someone to the lake or let me go!"

Blue took the tablet from Gray and whispered too low for Owen to hear.

"She's dying!"

They smiled pleased.

"This is all excellent data, Mr. Johnson." Blue stood up and inspected Owen's pupils with a small light and assessed vitals. "You didn't ask where you were today before we started. We've reached a critical point. According to subsection D paragraph four, disclosure rights are now available. Would you like to—"

Owen shivered and coughed back noxious bile. "Brain tumor?"

"No. We call this phase processing. This is your cell. You've been here just under a hundred days – our most challenging case – and we are ready to set your sentencing chip."

"What sentencing?" Owen blinked to focus through a haze that felt like the morning after a binge. The floor to ceiling glass wall overlooked hundreds of cell pods stacked one on top of the other. Each one silently shifted position to allow an active pod to slide into a personnel intake port like a candy machine.

"Mr. Charles Owen Johnson, you have been convicted of a crime and have been sentenced to a life in a prison of your own making."

"What crime?"

"We don't have clearance for the details. We avoid bias. It could be anything or nothing. Our job is to get just the right setting," Blue said. "Not to worry. The hard part is over. The sentence will be set for sixty years, well, for you anyway. For the program sixty hours. Efficient."

Gray had left and returned with a tray of small jars with liquid and presented Blue with a syringe.

"What about Deidre?"

Blue showed the photo paper to a lucid Owen; it was blank.

"She's no one. Your report showed a ready affinity for females. We merely suggested, asked the right questions, and you filled in the rest. You chose your fate."

Blue noted the time and injected into Owen's neck and spoke the words in a practiced tone born of a thousand repetitions. "When you are conscious, you will feel as if you are dreaming and will forget soon after, and in dreams you will feel awake. It will be all you remember. Not to worry. It's quite humane. You'll be hydrated and monitored. "

"I didn't choose...I didn't..." Owen slurred.

Gray changed the small blue monitor on the wall from ninety-nine to a blank screen, prepared the cot behind the chair, replaced the destroyed pillow, and arranged the ragged red slippers the prisoner had become attached to. "Reset ready."

"Good. Make note to increase the paralytic sedatives, we don't want a repeat of this morning."

After a few minutes when Owen's head bobbed, the two positioned themselves on their marks. "Let's use the last script to induce the chosen scenario." Blue waited for the digital alarm to chime and the recording to begin. He spoke in a low tone. "Find who, Owen? Find who? Deidre?"

Owen stuttered and couldn't hold his head up. He tried to stand from the chair, but the restraints immobilized him. "Deidre. Gone — lost her."

"How do you think you lost her?"

"Don't know. Don't know. Should I know? I didn't mean to lose her. I didn't mean to! I was watching. I was!" Owen sniffled and struggled. "The lake…"

"We know you were watching. You watched her for a long time. Is that right?"

"Yes—yes, I did. I've been watching. She's—in the water—"

"That will be all for now, Owen."

They unbound Owen and dragged him to the cot.

"Please…don't put me back…"

∞

A ball bounced.

One-ery, two-ery, dickery, Dan. Whack-a-mole, crack-a-mole, dockery, Pam. Theivery, dandy, step-in-time. Humbledy, bumbledy, ninety-nine. Oh, you, tea, out. You must go out!

Silence.

Owen ran to Deidre, but the out was silent, and the unrolling red ball was the brightest spot on the pavement…

CHAPTER EIGHT

Amaranthine

"WHAT'S ON YOUR MIND?" He asked the right questions, but I made him wait.

Someone had taken great care selecting the office furniture to coordinate with the warm, homey tones. The cornflower blue couch, softened from many behinds, sank deliciously when sat upon.

A hug for your ass, I thought.

A handmade quilt and hand-knit blanket, both worn at their edges and entangled in each other, clashed and vied for attention. The green wingback chair looked as if an old grandfather should have been puffing on a pipe, peering over wire rims. Instead, a man of forty years with a brown sand complexion dulled by office work rested there with his legs crossed. By all appearances we might have been the same age and sat next to each other in grade school. I knew the contours of his face well, even the place where the cheek mole had once been.

Cheeky rabbit. What game is he playing?

I studied the lace curtains covering the high, broad windows. The shadows of the bars crept through them and were cast upon the floor like a fine print that warned: For quality assurance this conversation may be recorded.

"It's a lot to ask of a person, being alive all the time."

As the silence stretched, it became clear I wasn't going to say anything more. My newly-assigned doctor leaned forward and quoted, "'Millions, who don't know what to do with themselves on a rainy afternoon, long for immortality.'"

I turned away from the barred light and scowled. "Read my file, did you? What talents Wiki-Ed turns out these days," I chided, but his eyes crinkled at the corners and a half-chuckle vibrated in his throat. His predecessors, a parade of well-educated buffoons who tried to analyze me, had all forgotten how to be amused. They'd been well-versed in the art of the fake, humoring smile, but their eyes had never laughed.

"I use all resources at my disposal. But, tell me what you meant about it being too much."

His professional expression remained steadfast even when I discounted the inquiry with a single wrist flick.

Sly bastard's trying to one-up me.

"Not going to ask me about my medication? Isn't that the protocol?" I cross my arms, regarding him with a snort. "Go ahead, assure me that with the right balance the delusions will fade and my path to recovery will begin on a road paved with horseshit."

Again, he smiled and shook his head, "A lot of brilliant people have interpretations of immortality. I wouldn't call them delusional. I don't think you're crazy…just sad."

"Weary." I corrected. "Never dying thins and stretches you over the endless ages."

He regarded me with the open will of a child waiting to hear the family lore. "I'm listening."

"Are you?" I sank into the couch, leaning my head back. I twirled a lock my hair between my fingers, focusing on how a sunbeam highlighted the wavy reds among the curlier brown strands. The minutes stretched, the silence ebbed, and the shadows moved before I spoke again. "There is time enough to do all that you could ever want. To revisit places to find them changed and new again, and to relearn skills the passage of years has made you forget. You are relieved of all worry of your own death. You see the 'I wonders' realized and wait for the unexpected to surprise you."

He peered at me, tapping his fingers on the desk. "Many would call that a gift."

"It's shit." I drew a deep breath, blinking away the emotions that threatened to breach my cultivated distance. "You bury another relative and one more friend until you've lost count. No mourners left for you; no one to remember. You stop celebrating the life in your own children. Instead, you await their last day. One more pyre; one more coffin. Headstone or cairn? Ashes or bones? What does it matter? It's always the same. Alone in permanence."

I sat up, gripped the cushion in my fists and glowered at him. "As you endure, in time, the memories of those you loved will fade. Now and again, a mundane thing like scrubbing the toilet will remind you. At first, the vague memory will delight, but the ages take even that from you. And then…"

"Then what?"

"Shame that you forgot. You stop hoping that you'll find another like you. All you have left is to stop living because death is not yours to claim."

"Is that what you are doing?"

"Existing pains me less than living."

He drew a command symbol on a control pad. The recording device beeped before shutting off.

"Is that why you are here? Hiding?"

"My file says I'm here because I'm unbalanced. But one day, before they begin to believe the delusion themselves, I'll feign a full recovery." I let agony droop my shoulders. "I've had the practice. They'll congratulate themselves and release me—free to go and exist elsewhere."

"'I write of you to remember when time takes you from me.' "

"You found my diary. *Bo ka burro sima bo ta parsi.*" It took a moment, but he rolled his eyes the way he had when he'd been shoulder high. The world then had changed around our defiant little farmhouse, a last refuge from tech and city life. "You always were a clever boy, Levi Royce, with toads in your pockets and digging where you weren't supposed to be."

"So, you do recognize me."

"I'm good with faces."

He removed his glasses and admonished. "You didn't have to leave."

"I stayed as long as it was safe to watch my son grow up," I whispered looking away to focus on the bars to center myself. "I take it back, you *are* as dumb as you look. The beard doesn't suit you. Neither does the new name. Dr. Gerald? Really?"

He rubbed the unruly whiskers and smiled with the ignorance of youth. "A necessity to make me look older."

"How'd you find me?"

"An interesting case with your face came across my desk thanks to your former doctor."

"Ah. Intend to fix me and drag me home?"

His brows knitted together. "And to share the burden, Mom. Neither one of us should endure alone." He stretched out his palm to me.

In centuries to come, he might understand that time was too cruel for those who could not escape it.

I am sure he mistook my tears for joy.

CHAPTER NINE
Proprioception

TWO MALE NURSES GUIDED A narrow, reclined electronic gurney into the room upon which the body of a limp female lay tethered—thick padded straps fastened across her forehead, shoulders, midsection and each leg. Dark goggles and headphones obscured her face. A lifeless left arm dropped from its perch and one nurse put it back with extra care.

While removing the headgear, the younger of the two attendants spoke low in a calming timbre. "We're here."

Were it not for the rise and fall of the chest and the goose flesh, one might have thought he spoke to a corpse. The woman stayed immobile and loose like melted rubber. After a moment, her eyelids fluttered, and her deep brown eyes were inspected for pupil dilation.

A hover-cam whirred while a technician rubbed her palms together, wrapped her arms around herself, warming her fingers in her armpits. "I can almost see my breath."

She adjusted the spherical camera's lens until satisfied with the output on the visual display and set it down upon its triangular stand on the small metal table. "Dr. Soares, all set. The hov-mags needed cleaning. Shouldn't be any more trouble. Changed the settings to autonomous like you asked."

The doctor in crisp, blue scrubs placed a pristine, round

magnifying mirror on the table. "Thank you." She adjusted her gloves and pulled down the sleeves of the thermals peeking beneath the over shirt.

"What're those for?" The tech nodded at a large floor-length, tri-panel mirror just as the single door beeped and slid open.

"Dr. Rendon." The doctor greeted the man who entered and hurried the technician out of the room, ignoring her inquiry.

"Dr. Soares." Dr. Rendon lifted his chin in acknowledgment before setting a plastic box on the table. He shifted his lab coat over a thick sweater vest. "Temperature seems good. Lower the illumination by a third, I think."

The automatic lights dimmed. The display panel on the door shifted from green to red and slid open again. The hover-cam left its home port and ran a circuit around the room, calibrating and recording.

The nurses wheeled the patient to where Dr. Soares had motioned, repositioned the tri-mirror, and arranged the gurney to an upright incline. Once the patient had view of her full reflection in the tri-mirror, her muscles found form, and the slackness of her face disappeared as if suddenly pumped full of air. She blinked several times while the smaller, magnifying mirror was moved to better show her mouth which at once began to contort and spasm.

"Itch! Wen! Cap...off." The patient's voice oscillated in pitch and volume, random like an antique voder. Each word burst between facial tics.

The nurse, Wen, fulfilled the request while the other nurse began to release the restraints, leaving the chest strap in place. Once the patient's arm had full motion, she vigorously scratched her scalp. The uneven, patchy short brown hairs curled around her eager fingers. A fresh-shaved square at the crown got extra attention.

"Ahh!"

The patient's cheeks relaxed after a few minutes, but body jerks followed: a shrug of a shoulder, stiffening of the neck, burst of breath, a stretched arm, and twitching fingers. All movements quieted in the same moment, leaving limbs in a contorted position. Seconds later—as if pulled by a string—the woman's torso straightened. Each arm twisted and flailed too high before alighting one at a time onto the armrests. Knees knocked together and bare toes curled and clung to the gurney foot brace. The woman huffed like she'd run up several flights of stairs. Sweat beaded on her hairline and stained her white and blue dotted gown. Both doctors noted the time from first movement to last and engaged in an enthusiastic discussion about the itching.

"Excellent. Ready?" Dr. Soares prodded when it seemed that the subject had become distracted with her image—opening and closing her mouth, stretching her neck, and adjusting her posture.

"Water." She produced a robotic vocal with considerable effort.

"Kevin, will you, please." Dr. Rendon waved his hand while continuing to peer at the notes on his tablet. The camera device found a prime position and turned on its satellite i-cams to collect data from several angles. "I've been looking forward to today's interview. Dr. Soares has relayed some exciting developments. She says you wish to be called Nina."

"Yes."

"That's fine."

The doctors exchanged glances and Dr. Soares made an electronic notation. The nurse, Kevin, brought a sturdy metal cup and set it upon the tray attached to the specialized gurney. Nina's concentrated movements mimicked a toy claw machine: move the hand towards cup, open fingers, inch forward, and clamp fingers. Despite the cold, a bead of sweat rolled down her temple. Veins popped out on the back of her hand and the knuckles whitened from effort. She gripped the cup, raised it, stopped, lifted it higher, bent the elbow, and inched it towards her mouth. Once the rim brushed her lips, the movements became natural and effortless though the hand did not ease its pressure. She gulped. Wen took it from her, though he had to wait for the fingers to release one by one.

"Still trouble with force? Does the cold help?" Dr. Soares tapped her stylus on the table.

"Yes. Yes." Nina inspected the right hand and practiced opening and closing a fist.

Dr. Rendon dismissed the nurses who retreated to sit on chairs behind a partition and put on noise canceling headphones, so they would not be privy to any classified exchanges. If they were needed, sensors on the gurney and in the room, would alert them by emergency tone. "Try touching your finger tips to each other like this…"

Nina—slack and expressionless—put her hand back on the armrest. The gurney displayed the rise in heart rate and spikes in brain activity. She flushed. Dr. Rendon looked at her over the top of his glasses. "How about we start with what you were thinking just then."

"Punching your face." She had found smooth vocal control in the outburst.

"Why do you think you want to do that?"

No expression molded Nina's lips. Dr. Soares tapped something on her device and Dr. Renden sent his colleague a knowing glance. Neither Nina's outward appearance nor the data output from the machines conveyed details of thoughts or feelings.

"Tired of this. Tired of you. Tired. Tired. Tired. Tired. Tir—" Nina clamped her mouth closed to halt the repeat.

"Alright. Let's not do a test right now. How about some simple questions? Then we'll see how you feel." Dr. Soares offered. "Tell us about your dreams."

"You know, like bile that comes up when you can't puke anymore." The words tumbled from her without pause—near perfect in their construction until the final word where a stutter lingered. The tension in her neck, jaw, and angry brows wouldn't release. Nina consulted her reflection, trying to find the right muscles.

"It might help your sleep disturbances to talk about it." Dr.

Soares's indifferent note-taking and review of sleep data offset the gentle tone. "No more meds if you won't attempt to sleep on your own."

Nina closed her eyes and immediately slumped lifeless. An exasperated sigh from Dr. Rendon preceded a hushed whisper from Dr. Soares.

Silence stretched for five minutes and the camera shifted to standby mode until conversation and activity resumed.

∞

Nina's attendants did not come to her side even after thirty minutes. She suspected they were told to not interfere or the alarm protocols had been changed to thwart her passive resistance. She paled when a sudden panicked thought caused an adrenaline rush. They had the power to take Wen and Kevin away from her, but still she refused to engage and kept her eyes closed.

"You can't shut off your hearing. Have your tantrum. We can't make you talk if you don't want to. But if we can't get the data, your treatment protocol will have to change, and I won't be able to help you." Dr. Soares tapped her stylus on the table again. "It's not a threat, just a fact. Understand?"

Nina had been uncooperative before. The last—a hunger strike—had been on the verge requiring a feeding tube reinsertion. Nina had worked months with oral therapy to earn its removal and didn't want to be fed through a port. They'd always find a way to force her cooperation, but that didn't mean she had to lay down a carpet of daisies. She opened her eyes and caught her reflection. The feedback provided visual input of the body's location. She aligned herself with thoughtful precision and gazed into the magnifier once more. This time the spasms were confined to the head and resolved in under a minute.

"Good." Dr. Rendon snorted through his nostrils and scratched his moustache.

"Dream pain. So much. Fire, skewers, venom. Zap, zap, zap."

Her monotone words spat out in rapid succession, slowed, and sped up again. "Wanted to scream. Could not make words. Dark, dead, quiet. Worse than anything. Anything." She squeezed the armrests with both hands.

"Why can't I make the right *fucking* face!"

"That may come in time." Dr. Soares wore a pleased expression. "We've talked about that. Your speech is already improving. Faster today, I think."

"If I don't hear this voice, I forget how to work it. Why? Why? Why?" The question stuck and repeated, fading into spittle.

"Perfectly normal for your condition."

Nina didn't think they had any idea why. They always gave the same non-response which explained nothing. "Way-way-wake up in the dark. Hurt. So much…but…"

"But…?"

"Remember. A head. My head. Fingers where my ears are. My eyes…so big. No body. But, my body hurt? My arm. And something crushing me. Can't breathe. Can't breathe. Can't. Wake up. Wake up! What is it? What. What?" Her hand snapped to her chest to clutch her chest and pushed against the rapid heartbeat. "Did I…Did I have a heart attack?"

"Did it feel like a heart attack?" Dr. Soares checked the cam to be sure it hadn't missed anything.

"Don't know."

"You could be reliving the shock when you first regained consciousness. We have you on a large dose of analgesics. Were you still experiencing pain?"

"Medicine didn't work, I think. Always hurting."

"The mind can play tricks on you. We think minor seizures are setting off pain signals in your brain." Dr. Soares waited for a sign of understanding and Nina made a soft affirmative sound.

"We've been able to control the seizures and temporarily shut off your sense of pain with a z-chip."

"Is that why…the mirrors? The chip?"

"No. Your proprioception—a sense of body—isn't related. Do you remember that we've talked about this before?"

The thing she called "the arm" or the "dead arm" fell from its position upon the chest and Nina stared at it startled. She began to hyperventilate. "Why did it do that!"

"Reflex. Just a reflex. Just like blinking and your heartbeat. Just breathe—"

"It's not mine! I can move it, but it's not mine. You say it is, but it isn't. Why isn't it mine?" Nina's voice grew loud. It lacked the shrill panic she knew should have been there, but she couldn't make the vocal chords work right. She might as well have been standing behind the chair operating levers and pulleys to marionette the body and pushing language buttons to blurt robotic syllables. Blood rushed to her ears, warmed her cheeks, and pulsed behind her eyes.

"Listen to me, calm down. Deep breaths. You are you." Dr. Soares put a hand on the gurney and pressed the com to alert the nurses. "Kevin, bring over the fan. Set it right here. It still helps, doesn't it Nina? The breeze on you?"

Tears blurred her vision and her mouth ran dry. "Yes. What happened to me?"

For a split second, the fan appeared to creak and stunk of old wiring and dust, yet the object Kevin turned on was new, clean, and emitted a gentle hum. Pockets of air blew over Nina's exposed skin. When she closed her eyes, the body did not crumple like a rag doll. With the subtle movements of body hair, she could envision body position. No longer a disembodied puppeteer, she floated in an outlined version of the body created by the currents.

"It's best if you try to remember on your own. Keep talking and if you ask the right questions more will come back."

"Will…get better?"

"Considering your progress, we are confident there is a chance these issues will resolve." Dr. Rendon comforted with a hint of impatience. "Recovering the ability to eat and speak has improved your odds significantly."

"It always hurts. Always." As she spoke, her speech pattern found refinement, although the monotone remained.

"What hurts?" Dr. Soares approached.

Nina watched the skin shiver and fear wormed its way through the body's organs. "Yes. Joints ache, but…don't feel it. Know they do or did? I think pain. Pain *is*." Nina stared down at a stranger's hands— heavy deadened things that either slept or buzzed with pins and needles. The trimmed nails on slender fingers had a faint lavender blue hue from the cold, a fitting color for a cadaver. "Arthritis. I had arthritis?" She stroked the knuckles with the other paresthetic hand, aware that the doctors' eyes never left her. "Swollen? Stiff…not bend. You—fix it?"

The eager looks they gave her made her uneasy.

"In a manner of speaking." Dr. Rendon sat up straight and pushed his glasses back into place. "You recall having arthritis?"

Where were the tremors when her hands were at rest? There should have been wrinkles, thickened nails, and liver spots, not smooth, taut flesh. Where were hers—the hands of a life lived and nearing its end?

Finally, she told them, "No. Just—what else…make hurt?"

Nina studied the thin body. She didn't fully recognize the oval features or the dark circles under the eyes, yet somehow not entirely unfamiliar. The skin should have been older and browner with a stronger red undertone rather than a deep tan. Then, in a brief flash, another person appeared in the mirror. A putty-jowled, hazel-eyed man not more than thirty, stared back at her.

Nina heaved until her throat burned.

∞

More than an hour passed before Dr. Rendon returned dressed in fresh clothes with his hair slightly damp.

"Ah, you're back. Took you long enough."

"Had a call to make." He sat down and motioned for Dr. Soares to begin.

The subject had been cleaned, set to rest and recover for a brief time, and brought back to resume the session. Dr. Soares perused the recent scans and sighed to herself over the indecipherable data. Every part of the brain fired all the time making it impossible to determine highs and lows or areas of isolated activity. It was like trying to find a night light in a white room full of floodlights.

"Cognitive functioning much improved and the aphasia is resolving. The grasp of language is stunning." Dr. Soares took a long sip from a tall, metal coffee mug while her colleague consulted his notes.

"The apraxia, the dysarthria...vanishing—" Dr. Rendon snapped his fingers "—just like that."

"And the memory perception in this one has an intriguing manifestation. Real or confabulated, Subject nine was describing pain."

"High level of tenacity. Perhaps that's why this one perseveres. Did you see the movements synch during the emotional outbursts? None of the other subjects can do that. We've barely been able to get random utterances and rudimentary motor control."

Dr. Soares crossed her arms and puffed air through pursed lips. "We should increase her PT. Encourage the emotional bridge in a controlled environment."

"Anything on the scans?"

"Nothing as usual."

"Do you think this is actual initial memory rather than fabrication?" Dr. Rendon ran his hands through his dried, silvering hair.

"Let's not get ahead of ourselves, Percell."

"Jaime, the subject can hold a full-sentenced conversation for fuck's sake!"

"Isn't that what we've been working towards? Reactivating

speech and motor control beyond reflexes? Repairing functionality? Encouraging adaptations and improvisation? This goes beyond reanimation..."

"But if it's the alpha..."

Dr. Soares shook her head. "The old Hava-STs sitting behind museum glass recall, mimic, learn, and make deductions...that's standard and not proof of anything. There's a driver in there; no question about that, but it's been through the protocol more than once. It's a clean slate like all the others. It must be a spontaneous framework."

"Maybe it is from a common pattern. Maybe not. We've seen subjects with various stages of muscle memory, but never this level of cognition before shutting down." Dr. Rendon paced the room while his partner leaned back and rocked on two chair legs.

"The subject could have been describing anything, not necessarily an alpha memory."

"But every time this subject awakens, we damn near pick up where we left off. Subject Nine doesn't start from zero. How? Why this particular one and not the others?"

Their study group handled all research and rehabilitation for all new body and brain pairings until deconstruction.

"Repetition? It's the only one that has stayed robust and had the opportunity to repeat and continue rehabilitation. Basic recall."

"True. Right. Makes sense. Explains the same preferences popping up in the previous eight trials. That beautiful brain still lights up like Vegas on the scans." Dr. Rendon rubbed his eyes and spoke out loud mostly to himself. "Very little degeneration. Same configuration with each reset. But, there's the name. Why an affinity for that name?"

"Again, repetition through the protocols. It's a rendering of Subject Nine, perhaps. Superficial recall. We've tested other names. There doesn't seem to be an emotional connection, rather it's familiarity."

"Unreliable readings. Any spikes we get out of that mess are still too erratic and random." Dr. Rendon sat on the corner of the table. "Let's review the data from the John Doe Protocol…"

Dr. Soares screwed up her nose. "That was a disaster—almost lost Subject Nine."

John Doe had been a male body, female brain grouping. The project had three main phases of oversight: the body, the brain, and the study. The blind coded assignments prevented bias or selection influence by those holding the patents, contracts, and copyrights.

"Once the emotions level out, we need to confirm if there is alpha recall activity."

Dr. Soares rubbed the stiffness from her neck and shoulders. "We don't have enough to presume there are alpha memories. Let's just stop trying to root out the glitch for now and follow it for a while. Look at the progress just today. The subject tried to make expressions, showed heightened distress, and employed more planned defiance. What are the odds of finding another pairing that works this well?"

"Not likely in my lifetime and I'm halfway out." Dr. Rendon agreed. "We have to be cautious in the reports I don't want this subject to get reclassified and reassigned. Right now, we aren't drawing too much attention. Let's keep it that way. I prefer my mind intact. I don't want a repeat of the Felden Research."

"Damn shame that was." Dr. Soares wiped stress away from her mouth with a damp palm. "Okay, we stick to the physical tests. Maybe explore the possibility of reading comprehension. Let's not push too hard; we almost lost connection a few times there. We'll do psychiatric evaluations discreetly. We won't record non-standard questions."

"Right, nothing conclusive. Give them enough to keep them excited. We've produced so we've got some stall time."

Dr. Soares accessed her private link on an alternate, secure device.

"I'll edit today's recording. Make sure that the attendants and that tech take their mem-blocks and have a full turn of REM sleep before they leave today."

∞

Nina twitched. Dr. Renden sent a message through his comm. The two nurses re-entered the room and tended to the patient already there—but ignored—resting in a reclined position. Her hair had been brushed to flatter and cover the shaved spots as much as possible. One of the nurses, Kevin, had suggested less clinical attire would have an influencing effect on a cooperative disposition. Instead of a gown, she'd been dressed in a bright red t-shirt and comfortable gray checkered pants. They removed the noise canceling head seat, set the electronic gurney into a chair configuration, made comfort checks, and moved away to sit in the farthest corner behind the partition.

The doctors waited for the subject to orientate and to gain control.

"How are you feeling? Ready to start again?" Dr. Soares said.

"Yes." She hesitated. "Before…in mirror…and saw this body…"

"You mean yourself."

"When…see…thought I saw another face—Not this one." The more her mood reached a deep melancholy the more her voice found a near normal pitch.

"Oh? Describe it for us."

Nina did not answer immediately. "Don't know. Threw up." Although she could let go of the puppet strings and appear catatonic, she could not stop the heart from thumping.

"The microseizures you have sometimes can distort your perspective. Because you can't feel your body position, you might perceive yourself—like you said—as having only a head or experience parts of you being in a different spot. Some people see impossible things. Talking hats or cartoons sitting on their foot. That sort of thing."

They told her about hallucinations and the fillers the brain put into memory gaps, but to Nina it had felt real. She hadn't told them what had caused the nausea—the man in the mirror. The stubble on the neck and chin even itched. Nina had had the compulsion to try and rip the face apart with her bare hands to get out of it.

A welling up of inexplicable rage caused her biceps to contract and tremble. A clenched fist slammed down on the table, making everyone jump. Nina yelped. "I didn't do that!"

"It's fine." Dr. Rendon said after composing himself. "These spasms may diminish over time. No more questions for now. Let's just do some exercises. I'd like to test your finger control with these marbles."

∞

Kevin entered the restroom and slipped into the corner stall. The wall *plastcine* covering had peeled off along the ceiling edge, revealing a word: *Observi*. Kevin snorted amused. He counted four up from the floor behind the toilet, and five from the corner, and removed the tile, revealing a small cloth bag with three plastic scan resistant capsules. In one, he placed a memory chip (which had the day's recording) and swallowed it. He wanted to be sure he remembered events after the usual mem-block. He was gone only for a few minutes—time enough for Wen to have finished his conversation with the doctors about the changes in the shift schedule.

Wen nodded when Kevin joined him, and they escorted the gurney as it wheeled itself along an invisible line on the floor. "Hey, man. They're upping the dose this time. Might want to take a couple of aspirin. Headache'll be a bugger."

"They keeping us over?"

"Nah, it'll be fine. They're concerned about residuals." Wen nudged Kevin's shoulder. "Don't worry about it. Nothing worth remembering about this job. Besides, pay's good and you never bring your work home."

"Yeah, but it can't be good to scramble us like that."

"Hell, we signed the contract. Look, I been doing this type of gig for years." He tapped his head. "Sound as ever. The headache's nothing. Steady job? My Hecktor and my kids taken care of? That's worth it."

Kevin gnawed on his thumbnail which had been worn to a nub. He thought of his wife and the suspicions he had that her death had been helped along for the sake of projects and profits. With the advances in biotech, hemorrhage on the operating table shouldn't have happened, and any routine intake full body scan should have picked up an aneurysm. When he started investigating rumors and similar cases of suspicious death, he discovered the rabbit hole ran deeper than he could handle.

"I don't know, man. I read that the mem-tech was stolen or reverse engineered or something. Doesn't seem right."

Wen laughed, his narrow, dark eyes amused. "Shit, I forget how young you are. What does it matter? True or not, that went down long before my time and yours combined. Relax, it's no big deal."

"If it's so safe, why the waivers? Why doesn't everyone do it?"

"Copyrights and money is like death and taxes. Keep your head on straight. When you get home go to a hot spot, have a brew, and find a date who wants to screw you sideways. You need it."

"Right."

Kevin didn't stop chewing until his nailbed bled. There were always security scans coming in, but the exit scans were randomized via a glitch no one had noticed yet thanks to budget cuts and an overworked tech-head. He hoped the capsule didn't dissolve before he could get out. If that happened, they'd erase more than his shift.

∞

Nina watched the lights on the wall through squinted eyes. They appeared to strobe as she was wheeled down the hall in a seated position. She trembled on the inside though the body showed no outward movements save for an occasional involuntary finger flick or ankle twitch.

"Hey, take your meds and head home, Wen. I can handle this."

"You sure?" The older man paused. "It'd be nice to get home

early."

"Yeah. I got it."

Retreating steps and the occasional beep from a display panel cut the silence in the hall. Kevin guided the chair slowly on the quiet wheels, looked down at the sensory headset on Nina, then moved a thumb discreetly to turn it off. The visor had been over rotated so that Nina's eyes could peer through the crack and at the small side mirror mounted on the chair.

"Could you hear?" Kevin whispered so his voice didn't carry. When she had been returned to the testing room, he had not turned on the sensory deprivation gear. Opportunities like that were few and far between. Today's mishap had been a lucky one.

Nina spoke words devoid of color, but in a quiet volume that took all her focus to maintain. "Yes. They worry...alpha memories. Why is important?"

"You aren't supposed to remember."

"Why! What am I not—to remember? I thought they—fix me."

"I told you they aren't. You're a project."

"Don't understand. Why is this bad—I remember?"

"Do you remember more?"

Her short-term memory worked in fits and starts. "Not sure. Don't feel...right. I think I am old. Was I old?"

∞

Kevin stopped the chair and pretended to tighten the straps and administer care to a crooked foot to steal more time to talk. They were in the same camera dead zone as the day he'd shown her the antique, turquoise cameo necklace—a family heirloom. He had dangled it just inches from her nose and her eyes opened wide and she grabbed it without any trace of the robotic movements. "Why do you have my locket?" she had blurted, perfect.

He'd presumed that he'd found his wife alive by dumb luck and applied for a job that wiped his memories every night, just to be near her. The stress of too much information at once had set her back.

This time he'd been careful to proceed slow and cautious. But that day, he'd been hoping for any faint glimmer of recognition after trying for six months. Full sentences from a near-mute had almost made him soil himself. Kevin had wiped his tears with his sleeve and fought to hold back the relief and joy that made his insides churn. "You remember it!" he'd said.

"Yes. Bought-bought-bought it. See? Inside, me and…and…and…" She'd struggled to string the words together. A mouth frozen into a grimace and uncontrollable blinking had deteriorated into rapid tics. When the episode ceased, animation had waned until Kevin had brought the side mirror closer. "Found it. Old things store. Fixed it. Fixed…fixed…"

"No, babe, you didn't buy it. This cameo, it passed to you." He'd known the story of the family's grand matriarch, Kaira.

The hand that had snatched the necklace so deftly had dropped into her lap lifeless. "No. No. No. Bought. Lock—locket. Opens. Press—slide up. Did I lose it. How? How? How?" It had taken ten minutes for her to utter all the words and by the end she had been sweating and gasping.

He'd pressed the cameo image with his thumb and pushed to slide it open. It gave way, he'd fumbled. A dried purple blossom had fallen out, revealing tiny picture of a smiling woman and man.

She pointed. "Me? Yes. Me."

Kevin had questioned her for several minutes more, his heart sinking with each reply. After he'd put the flower back and closed the locket, a noose of despair constricted his hopes and assumptions.

Kevin plied her with inquiries for months when the opportunity presented itself, even delving into the family lore, searching anything to refute the truth he didn't want. He'd been wrong. She wasn't his wife—not all of her anyway.

He'd peered at her soon after, eyes wide, and breathed. "*Fuck me*, what did they do?"

And here he stood, again, inches from his love's face, pretending to adjust a strap and stealing moments. Her scent still made the hairs at his nape stand up. The mind wasn't hers, though, it was the brain of a woman that he knew only from photos in the family cloud. A relative, an organ donor, who had lived generations ago. He prepared to put her back into the dark—storage, they called it.

There would be no grand jailbreak.

Any leaked exposure would mean she'd be destroyed.

He hung his head.

"Wife died? Yes? Sorry…gone…sorry."

Kevin tripped on his feet, startled at her words. He sniffed and guided the chair down the empty hall lined with doors with small square windows. "We weren't married. Never got the contract."

"No matter."

They turned left toward the second to last door and it slid open. "Alright, let's get you to bed."

"S-s-…sorry."

"I know." Acceptance and hope softened his voice. The foundations from their past conversations had taken root and she was retaining tidbits. Not much, but a start.

"Am I dead, too?"

Kevin paused and risked a confirmation. "Supposed to be."

"You know…me."

"We've never met outside this place."

"You know…who I am."

"I know of you. Yes."

"Tell?"

"I did." He wheeled her inside and lifted her from the chair and away from the mirror, causing her to lose the power of speech. "Many times."

Her eyes followed his movements. They could not talk anyway; the next shift monitored the room with video, audio, and data feeds. Kevin placed her on the bed, arranged her body just so, and turned the headset on. Others would monitor her throughout the night but would not enter the room unless a problem manifested. They preferred her blanked out in the mornings: no contact, no sounds, no visual stimulation for ten to twelve hours. They also would not check the apparatus beyond turning it on or off, so the data chip he'd inserted would go unnoticed. Isolated from the network, its detection wasn't a concern.

For almost a year, he'd removed the recording chip from the headset on his shifts and smuggled it out. All they would find now were pictures and movies from the outside. He couldn't abide letting her wither in the dark void when she could not see her body to move—the one cruelty, one wrong, he could put right.

A female voice broke the silence from the intercom. "See you tomorrow, Kevin."

"Night."

CHAPTER TEN
The Arena

RESCUE WON'T COME BUT I'M not really helpless. Small scalp wounds gush. If you smear it and feign injury like a bird leading a predator away from the nest, someone will lust for the bait. Already an eager foe has broken away. When he raises his trident to strike, I'll beg and weep and then slice his Achilles tendon with the shard cupped in my palm.

Many have already fallen in the arena: running, screaming, or fighting back with a ferocity that earns them points against skilled, armed opponents. The penalty for participation refusal is a torture more fearsome than a sword to the gut. My owner, Jaqquer, will punish me on principle, win or lose.

I fear nothing.

I keep small and stay mobile.

The fresh tattoos on my face—identifying my ownership—pains. I can't let the Netter or the others flank. My bare, upper back burns against the rough wall. Nox like me get an olive tank, fitted trousers, and light shoes. No armor. If I want protection and a decent weapon, I must take it.

The announcer's voice booms from the projection dome above. My collar issues a nerve-searing, snapping charge. Incentive. I squeal but refuse to move.

Entertained masses press their screen buttons from their domiciles and select their favorite lambs. The collars on another woman and two men glow crimson—extra points bestowed by popular vote. Sometimes the faceless who watch and categorize us as unworthy of status might choose the strongest or the one they despise. All whims and bent ethics.

"You're making it worse." The Netter looms, his voice muffled beneath the brilliant, plumed helmet.

I feel no pleasure when his tendons roll-up like broken springs and he topples. I need his shin guards, bracers, and trident. He has no shield. The rest of his Neptunian gear is useless to me. I had hoped to lure the woman, the Hoplon, with the spear.

The seasoned Netter sweats in agony but remains stoic. "Take the extra points."

Rules state Noxii can earn bonuses for stabbing and maiming the weapon's owner. "No."

"Idiot. Get out of the damn fodder. I've gone red, do it!"

"The moment I justify playing dirty, is the moment I deserve to be here."

My brother, through his juvenile machinations, revealed me to the authorities. If he were here, I might have to rethink my moral compass. Yet, didn't I look away from the trouble he'd wrought? Didn't I indulge and excuse the behavior that led me to this circus?

I wonder how much compensation he got for his sister? Perhaps, enough to cover his debts.

The two fighters left cut down the divided Nox in single combat. The biggest, a Secutor, wore heavy armor, but the preoccupied woman was a lesser fighter with an exposed back. In fodder battles, my tier are targets. Upper fighters don't attack each other. She wouldn't be looking over her shoulder.

Nox are supposed to lose.

The trident's spikes slip between the most vulnerable vertebrae and the Hoplon drops, joining ten other bodies.

It'll heal. We'll all regenerate and brawl another day. Our fellow citizens put us here because they are afraid. They say immortals are dangerous because ordinary death cannot grip us: *See how they kill each other? It doesn't hurt them. They aren't human. What can stop them? They are a scourge.*

My collar glows platinum with approval—a glut of points will be awarded if I am dispatched.

I haven't exhausted myself with futile tactics and had a long rest between evasive maneuvers. Stealth and surprise serve my strengths, but I can't take on multiple opponents head-on. The Noxii stare confused and step forward, eyes on my collar. The Secutor trudges from the carnage at the far side, and I move back to avoid being surrounded.

"We can beat him together."

One rushes me. "You're worth more."

"Don't want another round in *The Gray.*" Their faces contort with memories of discipline by sensory deprivation.

I don't share their sentiment. Jaqquer puts me in so often and for such length, it no longer holds sway. He thinks it terrifies me still like the first day. I welcome the solitude and respite from this captivity. The gray gives me time to learn patience, analyze the system's flaws, plan the best way to gather allies.

"You can't win. You'll be crushed, heal, and be back next cycle." I jog backwards. "He's slow. Run him like wolves then sting him like hornets. Points all around." They'd forgotten the rules or weren't told. I've been on the outside. All Nox win if every elite falls. Low odds; big payout.

They hesitate.

The Secutor's bears down upon me. His blow dents the shield and rattles my arm, fracturing the bone. My new comrades at arms swarm him when I collapse. Victory comes one jab at a time. The undying can afford the trials of patience.

My smile isn't for the spectators.

CHAPTER ELEVEN

The Fate of Undying

SIGNAL STATUS: INTERMITTENT
Missive: 4015
To: 01001100 01110101 01100011 01101001 01100001
Enter Code Key: ******
Processing...

Lucia,

Should I mourn for you? If a body croaks in the forest and there is no one to hear, would Death come? If you are well, I am glad of it. Yesterday, I hated you for the life you might have.

They've forgotten me and left me stuck in this in-between. Without a forward or back, what purpose is there in forever? I shouldn't have enlisted with you, I know, but what else could I do? You wanted to save the world; how could I not help? When it was over, what would you come back to? I wouldn't understand, and you'd convince yourself it didn't matter—until it did.

Who knew I'd be a natural as a relay jockey and we'd be working together? When I'd been chosen for Level 5, I thought what I saw in your eyes was jealousy. My anger wouldn't let me see why you refused to acknowledge my success and urged me to fail out. But, I've had time to think. Too much time. I know now that you were afraid, but not for yourself. I'm afraid.

Are you there?

∞

Reply...

Sender: 01000011 01101100 01101111 01110110 01101001 01110011

Stand-by...

Clovis,

The signal is weak.

The search consumes my every thought and I hope every day that you've repaired the relay and receive. At first, I thought you didn't want to leave your station for safety's sake or a misguided sense of duty, but too long has passed. Where did they put you that supplies have not run out? You must be restricted indoors because you mention nothing of change. Who writes eleven years of letters and doesn't mention the weather? The between and nothing and the past. What about your present?

What they did to you can't be what they did to me. When you were placed beyond my clearance level, I knew you were lost. I should have explained that I had a chance and took it. I was dying, and they made an offer; I'd've been a fool to refuse. You thought I was brave; you told me so. I wasn't. I didn't want to die, and I didn't want your pity. Simple as that.

But then the war touched us all. Is the dying or the undying the better fate? So many questions!

It's a damn shame we can't fully enjoy the lack of taxes. No bills or jobs, but no one to talk to. Not a soul but ours, Clovis.

Am I still me under all this hardware? I must still be human despite the hydraulics and wires if it hurts to think of you.

The Spring has come again, and I saw bison roaming. They paid me no attention. I think they know I am not a threat, but to be safe I power down under cover. A found a friend, Rex, who comforts me in the long days and empty nights. Someone loved him, once. No need to be jealous, but I warn you that his wagging tail is a force to be reckoned with. I have found a new body for him when his current one runs out. I don't think he will mind the transfer and I don't think I can endure without a companion.

Please keep writing. I will continue searching; I'm on the right track.

I have to be.

∞

Signal Status: Weak

Missive: 4315

Lucia,

Paralysis. That's my everything.

I move without moving. I don't think my fingers are here. Yet, I feel them in a way you feel your body in the moments between a dream and consciousness, when you see without seeing and cannot will yourself to move.

I've been robbed.

I can't remember the how. Isn't that strange?

Sometimes I can see a flash of light in the corner of my eye. Do I have eyes or just think I have eyes? I have no body, but I perceive.

I imagine the movement is you just out of reach. That's ridiculous. Is it still imagination if that is the whole of your reality?

I try to envision this nothing space as our apartment with the cracked ceiling and scuffed floors. We always had to prop the broken table with that horrible book. What was it called? I thought we'd grow old and have a few children. Your bravado and curly hair plus my intellect and knack for trouble packed into little people with no impulse control.

You always changed the subject. I thought you'd come around in time.

Sometimes I hate you.

I can see the empty desks and instruments through a foggy, gray water. Empty. White.

I'm empty.

Shut it down, Lucia. Unplug me.

∞

Reply: Sender

Searching...

Clovis,

I have said it three-hundred times and I will say it again. I found you!

Though if you send me one more pile of melancholy drivel, I'll have half a mind to put you into a cybernetic cat and let Rex torment you (he took to the new body and I think the hardware is better than mine).

I try to understand you, I do.

Before your letters, there was me alone. I watched overgrowth swallow city ruins, witnessed the return of vast forests, and admired returning herds crossing the Bourne bridge.

It's a bigger world with no one in it.

Beautiful. Peaceful.

I have almost worked out the override. It has taken a few upgrades and some downloading. Man, there are some things you can't scrub from the memory circuits! Anyway, I read your file.

They transferred you away from the relay station. Did you know that? No more cryptography and covert communications for you. They extracted your brain (not much else) and hooked you up to the Hail Mary network in the biorepository. Damn! You're the backup system to the cryo-cells. A blastocyst babysitter, darling.

No wonder I couldn't find you at any of the stations classified or otherwise. The file ends abruptly. They never finished the integration, so when you came online everything was still half-assed.

You know, it would be best to let them sleep. Who needs more of the past?

You wouldn't think such a thing. That's why they chose you. Had they finished the job, you'd be a proud papa a hundred thousand times over.

Perhaps I am wrong enjoying a world without static. You are all I miss.

Anyway, I've found an unpretentious artificial body for you.

Are you there, Clovis?

Tara Lee Davis

CHAPTER TWELVE

Aren't We All Machines?

"A RE YOU THERE?" FROM THE protection of the doorway, Nana waited. "What are you doing, Jaime? Come inside."

The rain pelted then rebounded on the wood deck. As the sun began to set, the solar lamps on the posts glowed. The seven-year-old girl in a green rain hat, coat and boots popped up from behind a table. She rested her chin on the deck table. She watched the three glasses marked with crude measuring lines. "It's an experiment."

"I see. Can't you do that inside?" Nana's shoes just touched the lip of the single stair.

"I'm collecting the rain."

"What for?"

Jaime blew hair from her lips and chomped her teeth to make the sound rattle in her head. "I –" she sighed, "I can't remember when I started collecting rain, but I think I wanted to know if all the cups fill at the same time or not."

"What a curious way to say that." Nana clucked her tongue. "You don't need to watch them."

"Won't you come outside, Nana?"

"You know I don't do well in the rain."

Jaime splashed her way back taking the long way around the deck to where the water puddled deepest. By the time she made it to the door, the sun slept and Nana was a dark silhouette against an orange halo.

"Why don't you like the rain?" Jaime asked while Nana meticulously dried and hung the plastic-smelling rain gear. Jaime poked a tongue through the hole where a tooth had been and curled her toes in the fluffy towel on the floor.

"It's not good for me and I don't like the wet."

Nana shooed her through the spotless kitchen to where dinner—kept warm under silver domes—waited. Jaime tapped the metal covers with a spoon and made faces in the polished surface.

"The other kids are weird."

"Such talk. Why do you think they are weird?"

"They're too happy and too nice to me."

Nana chuckled. "Is that all?"

"I pushed Sven in the dirt and he just laughed. Shouldn't he have been mad?"

Nana placed a staying hand on Jaime's spoon-tapping. "I am sure he knew you didn't mean it."

"But I did! Why aren't you mad at me? That was wrong to do."

"It's been hard for you hasn't it? Coming here? I think everyone understands that. Come now, eat your dinner."

Jaime slumped back in the chair then sank further until her bare, big toe touched the center bolt under the table. "All people are machines like robbies, aren't they?"

"A lot of strange wondering in there today." Nana smoothed her black hair with two hands. Jaime mocked the action by ruffling her own wild, brown corkscrews. "What makes you think that?"

"Well—mech robbies have parts that make them move, and people have parts that do different things to make them move." She lifted her arms up and flapped them down. "They need energy to go. They recharge. And they think."

"That's true. Some very particular machines can learn and adapt, but most are only programmed to do a certain task." A little floor robbie rolled by sucking up floor debris as it passed. "That one only cleans floors."

"But it learns where it can't go. Isn't that thinking?"

"I suppose…in a manner of speaking. But only a person could decide to quit and fly to meet the pot lights in the ceiling instead or create something for their own reasons." Nana took the untouched plates and tilted her chin towards the hall. "If you aren't hungry, why don't you go to bed? I'll come find you in a while."

Jaime oozed off the chair. She attempted to annoy the floor robbie by getting in its way. It only turned and resumed its task. Bored, she bunny-hopped to her room chanting a poem. "Who's behind me in the garden underneath the apple tree? Who's behind me in the garden whistling a tune to me?"

In the kitchen, Nana accessed an up-link: *Rain exploration on schedule. H10 inquisitive but showing signs of distress. Is it advised to—*

Startled by Jamie's screams, Nana left the relay unfinished and rushed towards the hall. Blood dripped from a jagged, two-inch gash on Jaime's left arm. Nana applied pressure with the kitchen towel. "What hap—"

"I thought it was me!" she sobbed. "I thought I was a robbie. I wanted to be sure. I don't want to be weird!"

"No, darling, not you—not you." Nana soothed and wiped away Jaime's tears. "You aren't weird, you are a little girl. Your brain is just too big for your body. Here now, let me fix you up."

Jaime sobbed and wiped away snot with her sleeve. "Am I broken?"

Nana shook her head, kissed her ward's wet cheek, and tended to the wound. After several minutes, she tilted her head thoughtfully.

"Shall I tell you a story? It's about how ten very special robbies, all persons with a shared dream, worked together and tried to build a human."

CHAPTER THIRTEEN

Tilt

THE WORLD TILTS.

It's like sharing a dream isn't it? I've been waiting. Oh, yes, you'll do fine. The confusion will pass. I AM talking to you. No need to tell me your name. I already know it.

Don't bore me.

A chuckle ping-pongs in your head. Thoughts key in like the rhythmic taps of a manual typewriter—sometimes getting stuck in a jumble of your thoughts and the *other* thoughts.

If you must, call me Gene.

You hear pills shaking inside a plastic bottle and the croaky spring of a desk chair. A *fwish* escapes its cushion and the metal grates. Reality spins.

Testing, testing. How's your reception?

Voices (not Gene's) tickle at the edges. Not where you are, but *there*—with Gene.

Look at you getting, all settled in. The last one had their face in the toilet for an hour. Don't bother trying to look around. Audio and sniffer only.

Static. Talking. Music. Classical. Static. "–non-stop classic hits from the 70's, 80's, and 90's. W–" The volume lowers suddenly. After a few moments, "The Closer I Get to You" plays. Gene's voice sings along off key.

"The closer I get to you. The more you make me see"—Hah! True. My mother used to say I sounded like a cat got its tail in a blender.

The world tilts.

Chair wheels roll along the floor. Your stomach drops followed by a light-headedness. Shoes scuff the floor to the musical beats. You swallow back your last meal. A lid pops. Something rattles.

Medication. Just some insurance. I like you. Don't want you fading off. Side-effects may include dizziness, nausea, localized swelling—yada, yada—and hallucinations—in case you were wondering.

A door creaks and footfalls shuffle on carpet. Up and up. Squeaks on stairs. An object plink-plink-plinks like the spokes on a wheel. A heavy metallic smell fills your mind until you can taste it. Familiar. But not like the metal of a machine. Organic.

You are the first one to notice that. I'm afraid you caught me with my hand in it. I got tired of waiting—had a little taste first before you showed up. But, I saved the best for last.

The radio fades. The stench of feces, and urine assault you. Your insides heave and lurch. A door closes. The scent swirls fade.

You don't want me to be upset with you, do you? Suck it up.

The *fwup-fwup-fwup* of a fan and the swish of wind whistles through an open window making the blinds click-clack. A sticky window slams.

Crimes shows never mention how messy strangulation is. They shit themselves. Piss all over. Don't do it indoors, amiright?

Your heart races. Blood rushes to your head. Gene laughs.

I didn't lay a hand on that woman. Strangling—not my thing. Do you know how hard it is to squeeze the life out of something? Better workout than Pilates.

Your temples pound and you try to stop—looking? Thinking? Hearing? Reading?

Ever had your windpipe crushed? Takes a while. You can revive and stab a son-of-a-bitch in the eye with a Sharpie. Better be sure dead is dead before getting cocky, yeah?

The wind rattles the windows. Rain raps the roof and panes.

A mind screw isn't it? You amuse me. Such dirty little things you keep tucked in here, and I'm only on door number three. Shh. I won't tell. Our secret. Did I mention that panic and pleasure make our link stronger? Shiny. Is that another door? Oh, what are you hiding in <u>there</u>?

The world tilts.

A sudden body shake starts a cascade of goosebumps from your scalp to your ankles. The springs on a bed bounce. *Squip. Squip. Squip.* You sink; you rise; you sink. Something sour curls up your nose; your eyes water. A deep voice moans. Not yours. Is it?

Can you smell his sweat? Bonds are unpredictable. Takes a while to settle on someone. I just have to wait. And poof! A voyeur like you. Hey, it's like Google isn't it? Oh, I guess you're right. More like Bing; it does throw up random shit.

I like watching. But I like when I feel you watching more.

I poisoned him, you know—after I made him kill his wife. Cut him a little, too.

Panic and bile creep up your throat. More anguished moans.

Sweet agony. Everything's better with you here. We're a team you and me. He displeased me, but I know you won't.

Will you?

CHAPTER FOURTEEN

Mine

MAY

IRINA READ THE SEVEN-YEAR-old headline: *Local Woman Assaulted by Husband.* She crushed the clipping and threw it into the metal wastebasket to join melting photographs. There'd been no reason to keep mementos, but she didn't want *him* to have them. Ripping and defacing had proved cathartic. The purge and burn had been prompted when a twenty-minute nap had become a three-day blackout.

The bitch thinks she can take me, Irina thought.

"I see you there." She spat at the specter who sat upside down on the ceiling like a demonic chandelier. The response was a rattling drawer and buzzing light bulbs.

MINE: the crawling frost on the window read.

Irina smirked. "Amateur."

Ravenous, she shuffled barefoot to the kitchen and stuffed her face with stale bread and leftovers until her hands stopped moving food to mouth. For the past two weeks, she was either in the throes of detoxing nausea or overwhelmed by insatiable munchies. Other times, a limb refused to obey.

Fury weakened and diffused the spectral bonds.

"Stop it! This body is mine." Irina growled, pulled at her matted hair, and stabbed the wall with a butcher knife until the tip broke.

A high-pitched ringing whined in her ear. The tinnitus episodes lasted for hours, vibrating the delicate inner bones. Irinia's gums ached and sinus pressure watered her eyes. The piercing tone turned to keening and then a shrill cry. It was her, Irina knew, trying to get in.

MINE, blared in Irina's head.

She rose upon her tip-toes when icy fingers curled around her neck and squeezed from within just before a weight pushed her down to the floor. Irina pressed her fist to her chest to quell the tightening panic. She ran down her therapy list to rid herself of the phantom: ignore, look away, and yell. When she managed to stand, she grabbed the kitchen broom and attempted to diffuse the apparition with broad swipes.

It cracked the ceiling and grew a giant egg head with compound eyes and piranha teeth. *Mine*, it mouthed.

"Parlor tricks." Irina blinked away the migraine halos and tessellations. Rummaging through empty bags and pill bottles scattered throughout the apartment, she sought relief. Liquor, unfortunately, had no effect.

"You are nothing. Get. Out!"

Irina huddled under a table and rocked herself, unsure which of them had spoken.

∞

JUNE

Sweat dripped from Sondre Brannvesen's brow and moistened his beard. Hadn't he shaved yesterday? He adjusted the high-powered binoculars. The cottage with the yellow door had a neglected lawn devoid of lights, but he knew it wasn't empty.

Bushes had claimed the abandoned school's roof which offered a secure and unhindered view of the neighborhood. Wild grapes spilled down the building, obscuring the boarded windows. Weeds, poison ivy, and saplings overtook every crack, gutter, mound, and hole around parking lot.

He and his wife had saved to buy the little fixer-upper and picked out the bright door together. "It'll make the house smile," she'd insisted. But that was before the aggressive cancer, the failed treatments, and the seductive promise of a cure. The rotting ladder groaned under his weight and he jumped to the ground, avoiding the broken rung. He'd seen what he came to see.

After a few steps, the regret and heartache of the past seven years gripped him in a patchwork of pain, squeezing his chest.

He'd been weak, and he'd lost her.

Calloused fingers fiddled a worn firefighter's patch in his pocket; the familiar bumps in the tight threads offering comfort. He missed the job but couldn't risk a background check. Besides, the micro-seizures he'd suffered since the day he lost his wife made that work impossible.

Sondre's breath caught on an inhale. He couldn't move and couldn't reconcile the sensation of being atop a roller coaster before the drop, though his feet remained rooted to the ground. Stuttered heartbeats harmonized with the tingling in his fingertips. The ambient temperature fell several degrees, frosting the plants, chilling him from the inside, and whitening his breaths. A sparking glint tickled the edge of his peripheral vision and accompanied the odor of buttered cinnamon toast. He applied counter pressure to his throbbing temples with his filthy palms. The seizure overwhelmed every sense. The auditory whine of a hundred whispering voices deafened.

A vision of his wife drifted through a distorted, broken-window aura. Little zigzags of light interconnected around her body and cast fractals on a conquistador's helmet. An Iron Maiden motif glowed on her breastplate. The thought of his wife as Dona Quixote made a hearty guffaw crash into sobs breaking in his throat.

That brain guy they made him see would have put on his bored voice and wrote on his file: "a seizure induced irritation of the primary visual association cortices causing a complex hallucination compounded by acute feelings surrounding a compunction." Sondre could have told him the haunting caused the seizures and not the other way around, but that tidbit of information might have gotten him VIP access to a St. Martin's padded guest room. Head down and mouth shut kept him in the state budget approved "unbalanced but not a danger to society" category.

The apparition glided towards Sondre, its body passing through obstacles. Her fingers made to touch his face, and he leaned into the nothingness. The cannabis oil he took for tremors began to wear off and his hands shook. He considered himself fortunate that the precious memories hadn't diminished under the strain of visitations, though he was beginning to have difficulty writing and reading print.

Soon. Her lips mouthed.

Their ethereal tether overloaded his brain, but when the specter possessed him the pain washed away in a refreshing rush. The ethereal embrace made his body shudder. The apparition re-materialized and touched its lips to his for a split second. He tasted oil, heard a snap, and absorbed the sting of an electrical charge. His eyes widened, he reeled backwards, and the vision was gone.

Oh! That was new.

Hours later as he walked through the neighborhood, people gave him a wide berth and crossed the street. Formication, he recalled, was what the shrinks called tactile hallucinations. Sondre recounted every detail, unaware he was babbling out loud and scratching his tingling cheeks.

She was solid? Could it be a migraine side effect? No.

It all was coming back around.

There were people who understood and studied hauntings. Sondre thought most of them were just wallowing in horseshit, but he'd come across a support group (of all things) one night when browsing the pin board at a last chance liquor store. The lime green flyer had been new and nearly all the address tabs had been torn off. He'd decided that if the paranormal support group's promises of "you are not alone" and "we can help" came to nothing, there'd at least be week-old pastry and caffeine.

Sondre used the last surviving pay phone in the alleyway between the Bamboo Hut and Seymond's Save-Mart. He punched in his sponsor's number with his knuckle.

"Hey, it's me. It—she touched me! It's like you said." Sondre huddled and leaned against the grimy phone box.

"That's a huge step. Are you sure?"

"I almost pissed myself. I'm sure."

"Hell, son. I didn't think your plan to get the ball rolling would work. You prepared the kit like I told you, right? There're no second chances."

"Yeah, yeah. Got it all."

"I've done all I can. You don't know us if it goes south. Understand? Don't jump the gun. Wait for—"

"I know. I know. Wait for the signs; seize the moment."

"It could be tomorrow or weeks from now. Don't get distracted."

"I won't."

Sondre hung up and returned to the safe house.

We are so close, Irina. So close.

∞

JULY

Irina was unaware that she had pulled one arm off her flimsy wooden chair and cracked the joints on the other.

"Are you having a hallucination now, Ms. Lomba?"

If she hadn't needed the doctor sitting behind his egg-crate desk in the bargain services office building, she might have bludgeoned him to death for his boring, liquor-slurred questions. Though, one couldn't always be choosy. Finding a sober psychiatrist dealing with black market medication was a dark web sort of affair.

She licked her dry lips and scowled at the taste of cilantro-laced soap bubbling in her throat. "Yes." She uttered the word with an inhale that made her full lungs hurt. "There."

"Don't pass out in my office! Breathe." The doctor took a swig of whiskey from an old beaker on his desk. "Out. In. Now, try one of our exercises."

Irina closed and reopened her eyes, but the vision remained. Each blink produced a series of stills, and the wraith inched closer and closer until it stood six inches behind the doctor—staring silent and unsmiling.

"It's not working." Irina rasped through a constricted airway. The tricks had worked before, but something had changed.

"Listen to my voice. It can't harm you. You are safe." The doctor spoke in a low, soft, rumbling tone. "Describe what you see."

"A woman."

"The one you've seen before. Describe her."

"Yes. She's—she's wearing jeans and a shirt with an angry skull man on it. Barefoot."

"What is she doing?"

"She's behind you. Grinning."

"There, see that's friendly, don't you think?"

Irina didn't mention the apparition blew upon the doctor's cowlick, making it quiver a millimeter. The specter leaned forward, moved its lips, and the smile yawned and wrapped around its head. Slender scratches crept on the wallpaper: MINE.

Irina shrunk back. "No."

When the doctor waved his hand where Irina had fixed her gaze, the vision winked out. She crumpled into the chair and her arms dropped into her lap. "I told you the meds aren't working anymore. You said you could help me."

"I assure you I have far more experience in these matters than my colleagues. In fact, my sister suffered from a similar affliction."

"I doubt that."

Other licensed doctors she'd seen had done their tests. They found no lesions or tumors, no hormonal imbalances, and no unusual activity in her scans. She could have told them that for free. The talents she needed weren't in their tests—it was in their prescriptions. They had all diagnosed some variation of Charles Bonnet Syndrome (visual hallucinations due to temporary sight loss) and prescribed a drug cocktail for physical injuries and therapy to deal with the symptoms. The regimen had helped, to her amazement.

For a while.

Then, the insurance rules changed and no longer covered her condition.

The doctor perched his bent glasses low on his nose, trying to channel the professional he used to be." Your case is—challenging. You were hospitalized with some complex hallucinations."

"What I need is better meds." Irina snorted and hid her shaking hands in her armpits. "I lost my vision and hearing temporarily seven years ago. It's fine now."

"But you have night disturbances. That, together with the recent migraines, is worsening the symptoms. I've got something to help you sleep, but there is that other matter…"

Fuck this hashtag has-been.

Irina pressed her lips together and glowered, trying to ignore the apparition squatting on the desk. "It's not a hallucination. You got the meds or not?"

"I don't think you will get past this, Ms. Lomba, until you confront what happened seven years ago. Because these— haunting—episodes you describe can only come from one place. From within yourself." The doctor plopped a paper bag on the make-shift desk and Irina dropped cash. "Are you ready to look inward and face the problem rather than treating the symptoms? Or, I can just keep taking your money."

"Piss off." She snatched the bag and slammed the door.

∞

AUGUST

Sondre lurked on the rear porch of little blue house which sat away from the road. When his spectral wife had broken every light as he strolled along Elm Street the previous evening, he knew it was time.

Irina exited the back door at her usual appointment time and ran into Sondre who wore a satisfied smirk beneath dark ringed eyes.

"Boo."

Startled, Irina froze and Sondre pushed her back inside. The shove knocked her to the floor and—weakened and exhausted from the haunting onslaught—she passed out. When she came to, Sondre was straddled on her chest removing a needle from her arm.

"Please, Sondre, don't do this. It's me…your wife."

"You. Are. Not. My. Wife." Sondre grabbed her throat and punctuated each word with clenched teeth. "You said you would borrow her body for a year in exchange for curing her tumor. A loan, you said. Remember?"

Irina's expression darkened, and she spat in his face. She yelled but cold phantasm fingers gripped her vocal chords from the inside and cut off the sound.

"Feel that? *That's* my wife. *Her* name is Irina. Not you. See her?" Sondre motioned to the mute ghost—his Irina—who knelt and smiled. "Do you see her!"

The Body Thief snarled. "It's my body now!"

"Your new doc messed up your meds for a crate of scotch." Sondre wiggled the empty syringe. "I've read up on your kind. I got this from a friend. It's like…a body snatcher antibiotic. My Irina just had to be strong enough and you only need to die a little—"

The Body Thief bucked, convulsed, and flung Sondre off with an energy burst. Green and black bile flowed out of her nostrils, eyes, and mouth.

"NO! She can't have it!" Ravaged by retching, the thief rasped and raked at her neck. She crawled away, clawed the floor, and flung aside furniture before denting the wall with her head, collapsing in a corner.

Stillness.

"I can't help you, Irina." Sondre shouted to the quiet. "You've got to revive yourself or you'll be open to repossession."

The body's skin grayed, and the lips turned blue while the green-black liquid drained. Agonizing seconds dragged; two minutes seemed an hour. The windows cracked, and the kitchen drawers were yanked from their bearings seconds before the body gasped, twitched, and rolled.

"Help me." Irina's hand reached for Sondre. Her nose bled red.

"Is it you?" Sondre hesitated.

The black bile pulsed on the floor. It shape-shifted into a multi-legged creature with stalked eyes and dissolved into the house.

Sondre carried his Irina and pressed them both through the stringy, tar-like barrier spreading across the door. From inside, the vulnerable Body Thief shrieked. Irina liberated the flare from her husband's back pocket and ignited the fire starter on the porch—Sondre had rigged the house for rapid incineration.

Their nightmare burned.

Irina screamed herself hoarse. "Mine!"

CHAPTER FIFTEEN

Incendiary

A CROWD GATHERED.
Everyone kept a safe distance from the flames, their faces illuminated in an orange-yellow light. The fire jet burst ahead fifty feet and sent up billows of black and gray smoke in its wake. Yvette Barboza, dressed in her green-striped nightgown, light blue house slippers, and cold cream still on her face, clicked the trigger with strong fingers. When all quieted and only the half-moon lit the night, she stood still and stared at three ruined, charred bodies, and the mangled corpse of Mr. Wells.

Shivering and in shock, we all gaped, though some had managed to record the macabre event on their phones. A few more bodies and we could have had a fine block party.

"Where the hell did the old lady get a flamethrower?" Len, my neighbor, asked a little too close to my ear. By the stench on his breath, he should have still been enjoying his buzz sitting in his Hanes in front of the TV.

Len, didn't own curtains.

The cold reminded me that I was only wearing a bra under my wool cardigan. I tightened it closer to my body and pointed my chin towards the carnage. "Internet. It was a present from Jonas."

"Who's Jonas?"

"Mr. Wells. Yellow house with the big, bug-out camper."

"Who the hell buys a flamethrower for their neighbor!?"

"He's—was a prepper. They were dating."

"Who was dating?" Someone asked from behind me.

"Yvette and Jonas. Don't you people ever talk to each other?"

I had just bought the little blue cape a month ago, and it seemed I knew more about the happenings in the cul-de-sac than anyone now that Mr. Wells had been killed by those—things. I never expected to hear the frantic, high-pitched screams of someone being eaten alive. I'm not likely to forget it.

"Did someone call the police?" A voice wavered in the night.

"Line's busy," I said. "I've tried to call a dozen times. Emergency and the direct police—" My dinner began to churn in my stomach. I pressed my thumb hard into the palm side of my wrist to squelch the nausea.

"How the *fuck* can 911 be *busy*!?"

Yvette stood in a protective stance over Jonas' body. Her salt and pepper pixie cut still looked neat and tidy somehow. People began to emerge from wherever their minds had taken them, and a hushed, confused murmur passed from one to another. The rising stench caused wrinkled noses, hands to mouths, and dry retches.

For some reason, I expected those things to smell more like an autumn barbecue.

"Who are they?" Someone yelled as if expecting Yvette to know.

"Satanists!" Mr. Vincent said with smug, fanatic finality. I wondered if his wife noticed he'd come out of the wrong house with his shirt buttoned wrong.

The murmurs turned to high-pitched bickering

"They aren't human. I saw them. They had huge mouths on their chests!"

"Well, that's stupid…"

"We all saw them eating him!"

"Bear. Had to be a rabid bear—"

"Bears have heads, Einstein…"

I walked off to join Yvette and put a tentative hand on her shoulder. "I'm sorry about Jonas."

She nodded but didn't look at me. We shared a simultaneous moment mourning while we scanned the creatures' remains. They had long, muscular spider-like arms on knobby shoulders, a concave indentation where a head should have been, and a gaping mouth full of razor sharp teeth on the torso. The sinewy legs were lanky and robust. Their black, talon-like claws on five-digit fingers were untouched by the fire.

"There's probably more of them. We should arm ourselves. Jonas has more flamethrowers and other weapons," I said. I hadn't seen them, but he was a paranoid man who did not do things halfway.

Jonas' robe had been flung aside when he'd been dragged to the middle of the street and I covered him with it.

"I have a key." Yvette wiped the tears from her eyes. "We'll need knives, bats, anything. The bullets won't last."

"Ginsu knives and duct tape, got it. I can't shoot anyway."

"I'll teach you." Yvette patted my face and I felt the strength in her hand. "He liked you. Had you on his keeper list."

People huddled in small clusters around the blue-green glow of cell phones, trying to catch any news or get through to paramedics, the fire station, or police.

Jonas' voice ping-ponged in my head. "Buck up, get your head on straight, improvise, and get out of Dodge."

That old man thought he had a bug-out plan for every situation. Wish I could tell him he owed me a new Benjamin and a bottle of Tennessee Fire. We heard a distant blast of the emergency city siren.

I shivered. Where the hell were we supposed to go?

CHAPTER SIXTEEN
Marked

THERE WAS NO PLACE LEFT to go and the hiding place in the basement had no room for one more body. At least, that is what Leslie told them. She shut the door against the protests. The shrieking from outside grew ever closer. The front door banged and splintered; a heavy thump shook the debris from the floorboards above.

A face appeared in the small glass window centered on the door. The mouth moved, but she couldn't hear. Leslie smiled and shook her head to reassure the wild eyes. She packed chairs, boxes, and speakers in front to hide it. The previous owner had built a mini soundproof room in the corner of the cellar for recording music. He was dead upstairs. Lesley with an "ey". It had been more difficult to dispatch someone with a meat cleaver than expected.

Crashing. Thumping. Breaking dishes.

Her heart thumped in her throat.

Lesley—neighbor and casual friend. How often had they joked about never dating because she was Leslie with an "ie" and that would be too ridiculous? Middle names were out since that coincidence defied all laws of probability. Who named their son Marion in this day and age? It didn't matter now. Her favorite jacket soaked in blood lay over his face and the blue t-shirt she still wore—the *Star Wars* logo still new—was spotted with bits of Lesley. Dried bits of him flecked her cheeks. It wasn't murder when a crazed man tried to rip you apart, she reminded herself. A lanky, sedentary dude with asthma should have been the least of her worries.

It had been three days since the cleaver.

Three days since she'd had a shower or decent meal not scavenged cold from a can. Three days since the red dust that turned the air crimson. Particles still hung thick—suspended like brick powder—but had begun to settle out and coat everything in a rusty coat. Three days since the angry, raised rash around her wrist, neck, and temples appeared and spread along her spine.

The shouts and growls from upstairs grew more frenetic. *Two voices.*

The reinforced cellar door bulged under the weight of repeated blows with a shoulder or makeshift battering ram. She finished piling up old office chairs to bar the little room. Not so much that those inside—mostly aging women and children—couldn't get out. Not that she was a spring chicken. Forty wasn't old, but younger than sixty.

The nails began to give way from the hastily attached planks. The two-by-four kick guard helped, but the rickety stairs wouldn't hold the pressure for long.

Crack.

Leslie gripped an empty shotgun barrel like a club but switched to a small crowbar. She'd looped a cord through the hanging hole and tied it over the rags around her wrist. A weapon had been lost to a weak grip more than once.

They'd all gone mad. The men. They attacked young women first—out of the blue and en masse. Not all, exactly. Boys under twelve and some immune men here and there—one was in the little room. He had a rash too. Everyone in there had one. Rashes like tribal brands. Not as extensive as hers, though. *That can't be a coincidence; we're marked.*

Leslie had been watching the news reports on the red cloud the day it began. The silver-haired anchor had leaped from his seat and struck his female co-anchor. Screams had erupted outside. Uncountable deaths; so fast. The women, among those who's survived the initial massacre, lost it next. They preferred children but formed all-female packs to attack and overwhelm men by sheer number.

A man's body broke through the door and the force tumbled him down the stairs end over end. He fell on the concrete floor head first and Leslie heard the muffled snap of bone. *One less.*

She stopped wondering who the dead might have been.

His roving buddy frothed at the mouth upstairs. Though he came down three and four stairs at a time, he made it and stepped on his companion. He barreled towards her—sunken eyes bloodshot and shriveled skin hanging from dehydration.

Leslie's rash tingled and grew hot; the deranged man was unmarked.

In the last moment, he twisted short. The crowbar missed and struck the wall. He threw himself against a beam, stared dazed—drool dripping down his chin—and blinked. Leslie prepared to bludgeon. He stopped growling, sniffed the air, and stared at her—through her. He curled his lip and caught her scent again then dropped his shoulders and clambered up the stairs. His footsteps pounded above; his screams were swallowed by the brawl outside.

Leslie collapsed on a vintage curvy couch.

Three days; still alive.

She itched.

CHAPTER SEVENTEEN

Inheritance

MOIRA'S BUTT ALMOST SLIPPED OFF the chair when the disconnected phone rang. Her customer's knuckles cracked when Moira squeezed them.

"Ai, ai!"

"Oh, sorry." She released her grip and pressed her shaking hands to the polished zebra-wood table. Three more days until the weekend. She needed to keep it together. The black mouth of the antique candlestick telephone yawned from its position on a corner shelf.

"Everything alright? You getting anything?" The white-haired gentleman lowered his voice and glanced at the shadows. "My wife? Is she here?"

That phone, she swore it—

No. The old thing was her mother Lavinia's shtick.

"It rings for me," she would say. "You've got the gift and one of these days…"

Moira never considered that her mother had been serious. She presumed it was for show like the quirky, mismatched clothing, gaudy jewelry, and belled shoes. The shop did well with selling high-end teas (blended for each taste), hard-to-find spices, incense, crystals, and imported tonics. The spiritual services provided a healthy bulk of the profits, in part, because of Lavinia's personality, her commitment to satisfying desires, and not promising what she couldn't deliver. Tourists got a kick out of the phone when she whipped off the concealing scarf with flair. "Expecting a crystal ball? I could just as well use a quarter behind your ear," she'd say with a wink and a jingle.

Lavinia had a knack for reading people and extracting information. They both did.

Moira considered her customer and pressed a finger to her lips. "Shh."

After a few leading questions, she usually deduced what they wanted to hear or led them to remembering the location of an object they misplaced. She could have told this customer she'd had the answer the first few moments they were together, but most folks liked a story. If people got the answer too soon, they'd leave without tipping, thinking a minute of truth wasn't worth paying for. They'd rather put out for the fanfare and truth wrapped in a lie.

Moira's costume consisted of pajamas or yoga pants, so a compelling story and some dramatics were necessary to reel them in. She preferred comfort and had no interest in the fine art of costume. The uncomplicated presentation amused the younger set, and the addition of a kerchief and dangling plastic curler invited the seniors to comment on her unprofessional appearance. The routine was simple: Look incompetent, take them unawares, and slap them with a fact that gave doubt.

The old man clasped her hands in earnest, though his stiff joints and immobile fingers made doing so difficult.

"Hmm. I see. Yes, I understand." She graveled her voice. "Spic-and-Span for a rainy day? Does that mean anything to you?"

He furrowed his furry brows.

Sometimes Moira had to poke around for the right amount of vague and not fall too deep into her desire to get them in and steer them out. "I'm getting a feeling of toil…a brass handle. A cabinet?"

"Oh, devil! She always said I was useless with the chores. Hah! Where else would she squirrel it? Under the sink for sure." He crushed his hat on his head, plunked down the fee (and then some), and escaped at a wobbling trot out the front door to seek his late wife's slush fund. The old lady had had considerable luck with the ponies and bingo.

Moira locked the shop and set the sign to closed even though the sun was still up.

The phone was silent.

Moira tiptoed past the dreaded thing then hurried up the stairs to the apartment she shared with her mother, who these days sat in a comfortable chair looking at nothing. Lavinia blinked away the fog a few times before acknowledging Moira, who placed a hand on the ailing woman's knee.

The moments of pure clarity were waning. Relieved, Moira cleared the lunch crumbs and empty tea cup. Her mother had been lucid enough to complete a word search puzzle, too.

"Oh! Sully has just brought me back from a wonderful jaunt." She smooshed Moira's cheeks between her palms. "You're pale! What's happened? Oh! I see. That would shake you up, I think."

It happened that Lavinia often had the answers to the questions she asked. Moira tried to avoid it herself, although she couldn't help but know things. People tended to get cranky if you knew too much, unless of course, it was Lavinia doing the knowing. The old woman got away with a lot.

"Please, don't do that, Mom. I—" she threw up her hands "—I can't be hearing dead phones!"

"I tried to tell you one day it would happen. I've shielded you all I could to give you the normal life you wanted." Lavinia smoothed the scarf wrapped around her curls and adjusted her reading glasses.

"This is normal!?"

"Oh, hush. We are what we are." Lavinia sighed. "There are worse ways I could die other than becoming a mushy-brained infant. Sully helps. But he's right, you must take over now."

"Sully's just something you tell the tourists, Mom."

"Is it?" Lavinia kissed Moira's cheek. "You're stuck. It's time to see everything you don't want to. Can't be avoided. You're no spring chicken. I did leave it too long."

"Leave what too long?"

"I've been keeping most of your gift dampened, I told you. Which one of us is getting addle-headed?"

"The phone—"

"Did you answer it?"

"It's not *connected*."

"Oh, sugar, you are always connected." Lavinia shooed her away. "Go on. You know it's true. How else do you charm the customers with your cleverness? You know things you shouldn't. No matter how much you explain it away, there it is."

Moira padded downstairs counting her breaths in the quiet. The florist from next door waved as he passed by the window with is bicycle. Moira peered at the offending antique for twenty minutes, biting her thumbnail to a nub. She took the ear piece and unstuck her tongue from her dry mouth to lick bottom lip. Red beams fired through the windows; the clock *tocked*. She exhaled.

"Hello, Moira. Sully here."

CHAPTER EIGHTEEN
The Summoning

THE HELLCAT PACED AND HESITATED at the mariner's statue where the strip mall sign had fallen from its arch. Dores's sneakers slipped on the wet pavement and she rammed her knee into a post. The beast screeched and leaped. She swore, threw herself onto the nearest shop, clipped her shoulder on the ajar door, and landed on her army surplus backpack.

"*Ae disseptum.*" She croaked, barely able to move her cracked lips. She outstretched her left hand and an indigo energy halo pulsed from her numb fingertips. The pulse at first felt like the push from two opposing magnets, but shifted to a stinging, searing misery. The throbbing never went away any more. An aqueous wall domed the storefront. The creature's nails gouged as it tried to halt its pounce to no avail. It rammed into the barrier and wailed from the chemical burn that left its fur matted and bleeding.

"What's next, a harpy?!" Dores's arm ached, pain sizzling from her shoulder to her knuckles.

An old fan in the corner blew ash and smoke in a stifling swirl. Its blades, caked in dust spun with residual, atmospheric energy. Dores slumped against the wall and squeezed her fingers around the ache in her left arm. She tilted to rest her pounding head on a display case shelf.

The flower shop was thick with the odor of rotting holiday pine and cinnamon. The fog outside was warm, and the platinum sun twinned a full silver moon. Bright blue skies and the green of day had become extinct in the new world order of gray, cobalt, and violet

A dozen mauve rifts burst apart, pulsed, and streaked ground to sky. The haze coming from the tears had somehow charged-up people. Some more than others. Twelve hours into the event of the millennium, Dores had fallen into a crash course in conjuration.

Until several months ago, when the purple haze spilled through the suspended rifts, magic hadn't existed. At least, not in a form that anyone of sound mind could harness. The occasional talent turned up from time to time. A lucrative palm or tea leaf reader (fanfare aside) could analyze a person with uncanny precision. Such skills had been explained away: anyone with heightened awareness of micro-expressions and body language could manipulate a client's perceptions. Sometimes rumored feats of strength, stories of body-snatching, or bizarre unexplained events made headlines in the tabloids. But even those who believed hocus-pocus magic *could* be done didn't actually believe it *had* been done.

After exhausting scientific research on all things sixth-sense, Dores had resorted to the dusty books that hadn't been digitized in the school basement archives. She had pored over any title referencing sorcery, demons, or magic. Most information had been cobbled-together drivel, and circular logic (baloney, her Nana Eza would've said). However, each one had cautioned against opening gateways, circumventing space-time, and unravelling the fabric between realities. Whatever that meant, she wondered who the fools were who'd done it and if they'd suffered for their stupidity.

Dores limped to the workspace at the rear of the shop, unsure how long the barrier spell would last—minutes, hours, weeks? From what she'd learned over the last months, her powers were growing faster than her novice experience could compensate. She should have been making pancakes and bacon, shooing the kids off to school, and...

She didn't want to think about that. Instead, Dores wiped away the demon hound slobber from one of the books in her bag. She sighed over the bite marks and the chunk missing from the top corner of the survivor's manual, but *Summoning Magic for the Beginner Practitioner* and *Et Convocatis ad Idiotae* had been spared. She'd had to bury a rather nice hatchet into the beast's skull to save the volumes. Pity that she hadn't been able to remove it again.

She poured some old preservative powder scrounged from a cabinet into a hasty circle and made a note to look up defenses against harpies later—one never knew.

"*Venite ad me, custos, in adjutorium meum intende.*"

Nothing. The crazed howls from outside intensified.

Mr. Cera her Latin teacher would have been appalled had the old coot still been alive. She thought that she had come close to uttering: come to me, protector, come to my assistance. The foreign words required concentration and she had a hunch the language or conjugation didn't matter as much as focus, intent, and will. Kriolu and Gaelic, no doubt, would have produced the same results if she'd known how to speak them beyond the endearing insults and mild threats she'd heard as a child.

In any case, her invocation was safer than the book's suggestions to summon by name powerful minions of low morals and questionable allies. Real or fabricated, Busas the Grand Duke and High Prince of Hell wouldn't have been a wise choice for anyone to call up. As both her grandmothers (wizened by doing without) used to say: Sometimes a recipe needed improvisation to make do with what you had or what you needed. They couldn't speak each other's language, but that bit of wisdom they agreed upon.

After puffing out a long breath, Dores let her fear shake her fingertips and allowed necessity to alter the diction and musicality of the summons. "*Venite ad me, custos, in adjutorium meum intende.*"

For fuck's sake help me!

The stench of burned starch and singed hair overpowered the

rank befouled water in the flower buckets. A force sent Dores tumbling over a floral tub and into the far corner. The energy caused the veins in her hand to bulge, and she touched the walls to dissipate the excess. The moldy paneling groaned and shuddered, glowed white hot for a moment, swelled, and splintered.

The book hadn't mentioned anything about blow-back and…What was that smell? Marshmallows and barbecue?

She coughed into a half-laugh because it was all too absurd to cry over.

What did you expect, Dorie? Et Convocatis ad Idiotae doesn't exactly sound like an A-level grimoire.

The incantation—or rather the convoluted dead language—had successfully summoned something. Something stark naked.

That wasn't in the book either.

The being had waist-length, straight dark hair, hovered just above the floor like a battle-scarred Vitruvian Man. He lifted his head, stared through black eyes, and spoke in a strange, heavy accent. "*Cognitio, arma, vinculum.*"

It took Dores several seconds to translate: Knowledge. Weapon. Bond.

"The tokens. Right! Shit."

From outside, the shrieks and wails of inhuman things tested the weak barrier.

She placed a broken broom handle into the being's right hand, and a bag stuffed with a pocket English dictionary, Rand McNally map, and a fat military field guide to survival in the other. Printed books were hard to come by and she hadn't had a working console in months. Around his wrist she wound a twist of her own hair woven with hemp twine.

He dropped, staggered, and fell to his knees.

"I'd've brought pants, but didn't really think that clothes didn't mat—"

He glowered, speaking her language. "What is this!?" He swung the handle and it sparked against the circular protection barrier. "I am not a servant."

"No time to be picky. It's a weapon. More or less. You can use a quarterstaff, can't you?" Dores handed the nude man her sleeping blanket. "I didn't know about the clothes."

"Where are the Phylacteries of Knowledge?" His heavy accent caused hesitation between syllables, but as he spoke the rhythm settled.

"Books? I had a few more but the hell hounds got them. Lost a really good hatchet, too." Dores refused to wilt under his scrutiny. "It's all I have. I'd've stopped at the Allmart, but it looked overrun by rabid lamia. And, I wish that was a joke."

The books levitated, whirled, and the pages flipped. "Your gifts—inadequate." He acknowledged the twine with a disgusted scoff and peered at her.

Dores smoothed down her brown hair and tossed her head back. "Look, the instructions said the bond token had to be something close to the user. I didn't think to pack any heirlooms in the hand basket when shit went sideways."

"Amateur. Child. How did you call me in the middle of battle? The Overseers do not suffer fools. They will find you."

"I'm forty-two you arrogant snot."

You're *my* bodyguard now. Your former—employers—can get in line and take a damn number. I've got bigger problems." Dores tilted her chin towards the other-worldly creatures searching for flaws in the shield spell. She crossed her arms and stood firm. "What's your name?"

He snorted, and his eyelids drooped. "Death will find you soon, but you may call me Taiji Kyudo."

Dores slammed down a misshapen hunk of glowing amber no bigger than a golf ball onto a workbench. The summoned, she'd learned, was compelled to provide knowledge to the summoner. "What is this? How do I get the people out?"

Taiji straightened. "A lifestone. How did *you* get that?"

"How do I free the people in it?"

He laughed and scoffed. "You can't. It traps all the minutes of a person's life and leaves them with nothing." Taiji blew through his wiggling fingers. "Gone the moment they were chosen."

Dores grasped the stone to her chest, rocking back hand forth until tears dripped down her chin and her ears ached. Her powers leaked like ink on paper. Static charge raised hairs and snapped around objects.

Taiji furrowed his brow and rubbed his temples. "That is too powerful for charlatans. Be rid of it."

Blood flushed her face. Dores lowered her voice and clenched her fists. "A beast came to my house and murdered my family, so I ripped out its heart."

The ever-present power charge in her body seeped, flecking the paint off the walls. A tornado of debris whipped around while the fan buckled. The same invisible, crushing force pulverized a ceramic gnome and splintered workbenches. Sweat beaded on her upper lip; her ears bled. Untethered objects tumbled together in a wild, frenetic debris twister. The mauve aura surrounding her body expanded and intensified the summoning bond with Taiji.

The sacrifice that had been made for the summons hadn't been what the book recommended.

The boy… Martin…

No! Don't think about that. Not yet.

"Parlor tricks?" Taiji scoffed before he doubled over.

Dores's foot disrupted the circle upon the floor and the barrier spell around Taiji faltered. He pushed through the pressing weight and grabbed her.

"Can't…control…" Caught in the eddy of channeled energy, Dore's eyes watered and her arm prickled with heat.

The physical contact caused a burgeoning telepathic link to magnify into a frontal invasion of Taiji's mind. He witnessed through

112

her memories her struggle to survive in a fractured reality that had no use for a teacher, wife, or mother.

All she had seen and lost became his to experience.

∞

The past echoed and reverberated. Like a spliced film reel, grainy scenes flickered and jounced from one to the next.

A holoscreen broadcast breaking news "A decade ago reports of suspected bear attacks in…current resurgences have authorities…speculations of another aggressive rabies…"

"A red cloud has overtaken…first responders say…"

—*Winter snowfall winked to summer heat*—

The weather channel reported "…record breaking hurricane force winds…expect a deluge… flooding. Estimated fifty inches of precipitation across…satellite images show anomalies…"

"Mom, look! The pictures look like marshmallow fluff." Ian, pressed his sticky fingers into the sofa. His little sister, Maia, licked the table and squealed. "Can we have fluffernutters for dinner? Pl—"

The screen changed to the Emergency Broadcast System.

—*The lamp bulbs burst*—

In her office where she broadcast her virtual classroom, Dores's hands trembled and she lost her lunch in a wastebasket. Shelves had toppled, and objects whirled as if in a windstorm. The overheads flickered out and the green-screen cracked. The *Ms. Sabine Number One Teacher* nameplate on her desk console melted. Her boss led her out of the building. "…damn earthquakes…can you get home?"

Alarms and sirens blared. The electric cars and trams stopped in their lanes simultaneously. Traffic signals blinked and cycled randomly.

—*Street lights burned out*—

Maia squealed when Dores blew raspberries on her pudgy belly.

A cold breakfast waited on the table.

Flood waters drowned the kitchen. Taped and boarded windows shook. The sky darkened. The thread-thin tears widened.

The children cried behind their father's legs. Her horrified husband gaped at the hole in the wall and backed away. She had been wondering what use her husband was other than making himself an obstacle in the daily drudgery. Dores had been staring nothing thinking of bills, appointments, grading, empty savings, messages to write, the current chaos, the apathy consuming her marriage, and how much she'd despised the floral wall coverings. Stupid, dainty flowers as numerous as her responsibilities. In the next moment the wall sunk in on itself like a whirlpool. Trevor's hazel eyes accused.

Screaming.

—darkness. The hum of a generator—

Dores pounded on the cellar door. "Trevor! Trevor!"

Her husband had locked her in, barricading both exits. "Something's wrong with you. We need help," he'd said, his voice shrill. Her children cried, "Mommy!"

The city-wide emergency siren's tone rose and fell. Gunfire popped. Explosions boomed.

Shrieks from outside.

—a bare bulb pulsed—

The scent of sweet orange honey and butterscotch swirled in the stifling heat. Something else was there in the house.

She focused on the door, her babies, helplessness, and the abrupt end to Trevor's grunts. The air pressure around her body plummeted, sucking the air from her lungs. The door splintered out and away...

Trevor's soulless eyes.

Ian's lifeless body.

The beast, a moving mass of amber in a humanoid shape, turned to her and emitted a warble of triumph as it dropped her limp baby girl. Its malleable face smiled.

An unseen wall, a barrier Dores didn't know she'd conjured, locked them together. She shoved her bare hand into its innards and grasped the glowing heart that beat with the life force of her family. She could feel them there—each essence distinct, confused, and clinging to each other. They could be put back, she thought, heat seared her palm and the beast's shrill shriek perforated her eardrums.

The heart in her triumphant hands.

The creature dull, brown—dead.

Running.

Mourning.

Hiding.

Martin. Her former student—barely fifteen. She couldn't save him either. His raging fever refused to come down no matter what remedy she tried or medication she scavenged. The poisoned bites rotted his legs from the inside out. Together they searched for organic and magical solutions; Dores could conjure and destroy, not heal. At the last, he'd drawn power symbols on himself, and begged her to say the incantation for a summoning spell they'd found in a reliable book and had initially rejected… His hand grew cold in hers. The words… sawdust in her mouth…

No!

∞

An electric jolt separated them. Taiji didn't bother to dry his face. Her unharnessed power overwhelmed and crushed Taiji's thoughts; there had been no mutual exchange of experience. He held his head against the severe strain. Dores struggled to stay upright and discharged the residual energy through the floor, cracking the tiles. The air cooled and floating items fell. Their tether was palpable, but she had no room nor desire to absorb his past.

Dores shook off the memories.

"We might find supplies around here." She shivered and let out a steadying breath. "You can start with the hellcat that's been stalking me. I only wounded it. I wouldn't screw me over if I were you. I'm pretty sure that if I die, you—" She blew through her wiggling fingers, mocking his earlier response to her questions about the lifestone.

Her voice was as tight as her fist. "Get rid of them."

"So the bonds compel. As commanded." Taiji's pained

expression faded to indignant annoyance. He bowed his head and left, wielding the broom handle and a rusty knife rummaged from the floor.

Alone, Dores slumped into a corner and looked out the storefront window. The protruding veins in her arm and face contracted, returning to normal. The protective dome hovered on the edge of collapse and beyond the rifts glowed. Her nose bled.

She clutched the amber lifestone, which pulsed with the suspended life force of her murdered family and so many others, to her breast. She'd been too late for them, but it wasn't over yet. Taiji wasn't a repository of all knowledge. Hadn't she already done the impossible?

The unfamiliar skies offered no solutions. Lightening flashed.

Her chapped lips pressed together in a determined line. "I'll close them my damn self."

CHAPTER NINETEEN

A Bolt from the Blue

LIGHTNING FLITTED ACROSS A CLOUDLESS blue sky for twenty-five miles and buffeted the hot, heavy summer air, announcing my caravan's arrival. The thunderclap and ozone static quickened hearts and prickled noses. Though we will linger a single day, to the locals we've always been, and when departed we never were.

It's part of the glamour.

Beasts pulled and worked: furry four-tusked elephants, red-eyed aurochs, the great roc, and a pair of cockatrice. The barkers stretched their vocals while other carnies glammed their game joints, rides, and food grabs. Drab wagon facades shifted in waves to vibrant hues while the buntings clashed with garish lights. Feather-hocked, blue-eyed horses with metallic coats nickered.

"Still tryna take a brody?" Coraline smirked at me beneath her intricate, pastel face brands. Everyone had a unique visage, though some wore masks, too. Each invariable design, no matter the color or pattern, was an ever-present reminder of our curse and our obligation.

Coraline elbowed her cyber-goth companion who scoffed through a ventilator. "Watch it or you'll get ankled."

They thought my flop attraction was all washed up because I

117

didn't use magick on my rig for anything other than holding it together.

"I don't need to chew the scenery to get attention."

"You know what'll happen if ya don't fill quota, Victoria."

My stage name still sounded tinny even after the perpetual passing of years. No one knew what would happen; no one had ever run dry. Anecdotes and nightmares weren't truths.

"I'm righter than a dog with two peckers." I showed them the broadside of my short bustle until they moved on.

I cranked open my rig, replaced bulbs, and manually applied decorations. There was time aplenty for tedious handiwork, so I'd covered the facade in intricate, radial patterns of colored pebbles and glass. Souvenir shoes of all styles and periods which lined the track side by side, got a good polish. I oiled the red leather seats and dusted *The Ride of a Lifetime* sign.

Late afternoon, I had my chance to gad about town. My mauve and black striped skirt stopped at my knees, showing off my underpinnings. Folks complimented my lace mask and Victorian inspired ensemble, taking photos with their ubiquitous palm phones. Townies clapped and cheered at impromptu performances. I wended my way through the young and old and meandered between the fair and foul, handing out exclusive tickets to the noteworthy.

When I found a fat mark, I swooned. Among the slim pickings, I'd found bountiful fuel. My colleagues blinded themselves with flash and missed the nuances of deep, camouflaged evil. I could smell it like the sweet, heady scent of gillyflowers in a boudoir.

Quality over quantity.

I blew a little glamour on the red and gold tickets—a seasoning, nothing more—and presented them to the couple who'd caught my eye. "Complimentary." I curtsied. "Come? It'll be a night you'll ache to remember."

Their pupils glowed yellow for a moment and their bodies relaxed. Each nodded in turn, accepting the invitation and binding the spell.

After choosing a few others, I returned to my wagon to prepare until evening when the carnival lights twinkled. Since I knew the lines of my curse intimately, refreshing the missing strokes with makeup had become second nature and took an hour to complete. If didn't recreate each one with meticulous precision, the wagon wouldn't let me leave. The brands were how my accursed fellows and I identified each other. Charms, however, barred us from discussing our pasts or punishments with each other. They were supposed to be permanent reminders of our doom.

Permanence, I discovered, had a certain flexibility.

I was ashamed to look at myself, yet, how could I ignore the slow return of my unblemished face? Dare I think...? No. I'd learned the folly of selfish musings and avaricious wishes. I had drawn my lot and sealed my fate. I didn't deserve redemption.

At dusk, not long after the night cockatrice's crow, I attended to my first customer. An old woman, with arthritic hands and face contorted by pain, showed me her red ticket.

"Ah! Madam! As punctual as you are lovely." I guided her to the high backed, curved seat and pulled down the bar.

"Will I get to see? Liked you promised?"

"All fine things yet ever known to thee, from smallest wish, unto your heart's longing plea." I finished the incantation as she disappeared behind the curtains. The rig chains *clacked*, and the ailing seams joggled like the old woman's joints.

While I was waiting for the ride's cycle to complete, the couple from earlier stepped within the carnival's boundaries and a lightheadedness overtook me. Their tainted scent assaulted my body, bones, and blood in a fevered rush. Woozy and disoriented, I had to hold onto the railings. The man's voice, full of spite and misanthropy, carried over the crowd's hubbub and drew the attention of my colleagues. Ogling was free, but no one would dare pinch my prize.

The pair approached about the same time my first customer

exited the ride. Though her eyes were wet with tears, the old woman smiled. Her crepe skin quivered and she lifted her stiff fingers to her sagging cheeks. "Thank you!"

She'd lost her kerchief in the excitement. I replaced it on her balding head, tied it under her chin, and then bent to right the laces on her orthopedic shoes. Within my hand, I formed a tiny ball of gray magick and blew it gently upon her face. "There you are. A little something for you."

A glow returned to her rheumy eyes, her swollen knuckles shrunk, and she stood straighter. I couldn't prolong her life, but I could make her last months pleasant enough to enjoy with enough spryness to remedy regrets. I had to be careful. That minuscule gift made the workings on the rig creak and pop.

My elderly customer took a deep breath and the accumulated aches left her face. As she merrily left and passed by the couple who so excited me, she told them, "A ride to remember!"

The man ignored her. He busied himself with lavishing verbal assaults upon his petite companion who stared at her canvas shoes as she hugged her cerulean sweater. My temporary compulsion spell would soon be overpowered by his resistance.

"Come!" I guided my marks to the high backed, curved seat. "A sight to be seen awaits."

The man dragged. "This's a waste of time."

"Mayhaps, but can free time be wasteful?"

He plopped down, and the platform shook. "Hurry up, Daisy. Haven't got all day waiting for your ass."

"What will I see?" Daisy stared into space; her lips twitched.

"All fine things yet ever known to thee; from tiny wish, unto the foulest deed." While bent over feigning adjustments, I traced my fingertip along the sole of her left shoe to tag it when I cast the scrying spell. From the sole, the heart's mind and life essence were accessible.

I set the system in motion and they disappeared into the dark maw beyond the navy curtain. They screamed moments later.

Pleased with my offering, the ride tremored and sparked before granting me entry.

Inside, a single gaslight burst with flame. The seats held the couple fast. The ride groaned, rattled, and creaked. My silks rustled, and my shoes knocked on the ancient wood. "Not to worry. My rig only desires one of you."

Daisy's eyes were wide and wild. She squeaked, "Him! Take him!"

He panicked against the restraints. "What is this you crazy b—"

With a practiced spell, I pulled from his throat a green glob formed of all the nasty things that ate and rotted him from within and fed it to the starving gaslight. The ordeal left him disoriented, mute, and drained of hate. Guilt from all he'd wrought would plague him— change him.

"Shh. The women are speaking." I reached for the floor lever to begin consumption.

"I'll do it. Let me! I'll send the bastard to hell!"

"We send ourselves to our torment." I cautioned and tapped my fingers on the wall.

Daisy's bonds slackened. She sprang to my side and grasped the lever in a desperate fury.

"If you do this, your lot is tossed. Choose oblivion." My words were sincere. This existence I would not wish upon the vilest creature.

Her terrible smile cracked as she pulled. The invisible shackles ripped from their tethers in my back and pushed their way into her flesh. Ornate brands burned deep red and black upon her face. She shrieked and writhed. The enchanted shoe glowed and rooted her foot; she'd never again take it off. The last of my facial marks vanished leaving empty places where I hadn't applied makeup. I stood clad in soleless shoes and the garb I'd worn the day I'd made my choice. Sweat dripped down my temples and pricked my underarms. Tremors of pain shook me where the enchanted chains had torn from my body.

Unfathomable centuries had passed before I had grasped the

brands' purpose. Only selfless acts could unmake them. One could never undo a deed, but one could make unselfish amends and leave a place or person better than they found them. When Daisy cast her lot of her own accord and became Victoria, my rig accepted the exchange as fulfillment of my remaining debt.

"Forward, never back," I advised her, choking on my shame which had never diminished.

I led the dazed man out. Although a scoundrel, he hadn't done the unspeakable things that made Daisy sweet with the corruption of serial murder.

My painstaking rig detailing disintegrated and, in its place, a gorgeous display of vibrant excess bloomed more glorious than all others.

Ground to sky lightning cracked and the carnival dematerialized.

Never was and somewhere else.

CHAPTER TWENTY

The Lies that Bend

I DREW MY WOOL AND fur cloak closer to hide my quivering hands and defiant posture. My heart wished to be somewhere else and speak other words.

"This dotter is grateful for your wisdom in this betrothal, Papa."

I stared straight into his eyes and drove the lie home.

The magistrate cob roller who had come to oversee compliance glowered from the doorway. My mother tipped her head, frowned, and corrected me to use the more formal "Foder" or "Ser". The invader's vile language had infested our native tongue over the past six years like chiggers. The brutish words lacked; they left a bitter sting on my tongue and a wad of bile in my throat.

"Gud! There, you see?" Papa said to the disapproving magistrate, though he held my gaze.

His naked face and shorn hair disturbed me and churned my innards. The foreigners had forced all our men shear and shave to show loyalty, display civility, and acquiesce to conformity. Now, the biting winds chapped their bare cheeks, and strange faces had replaced kith and kin. It was all wrong. I missed braiding Papa's weathered locks by the hearth and beading his beard as he told me stories of our ancestors (of the great creatures they hunted, the iron beasts they charmed, and the empyreal cities they built). One day, our elders said,

123

we'd rediscover the old ways and return to the skies and explore fathoms beneath the seas. With most of the elders and leaders dead, my parents were among the few who remained who knew the wise tales.

"May I have leave to visit the ancestors?"

My mother clasped her hands tighter and pressed them to her lips. "You should pray to –"

"Ach, Grineld, let it be." Papa admonished with a gentleness that made the magistrate frown.

She bowed her head and glanced askance out of the window to the darkening skies.

Where had my mama gone? We women were all to clothe ourselves in garb drabber than the evening mid-winter mists on gray rock and to coil our hair so that even a breeze would forget we stood in it.

My mother had once decorated her tresses with plaits, twists, and purple shells. Many hours she had toiled in the winter to weave beautiful garments of dyed wool and hemp.

Perhaps, I thought, my mother sought worth in obedience to protect herself now that women could not carry even a sharpened stick without punishment. It'd be better to watch her fall upon a spear than to witness her dignity drown under a tide of bootlickings.

Papa motioned to wave me away, but then he held my gaze and clasped my arms. His roughened hands left earnest heat prints even through my furs. "Bren, my dotter, heed the weather. I had pains in arranging your betrothal before the squalls. Say your farewells, for tomorrow you go where we cannot."

Did he waver at the word farewell? Had he lingered too long at "before"? Was that hope there in the deep dark of his eyes?

When I nodded at the reassurances, the tension melted from Papa's face and his shoulders loosened. His crow's feet crinkled.

I bowed my head in the new way, though I yearned to throw myself into their arms and have us all embrace as we once did. Even with the cold sting of a dozen lost children, they had always had laughter to gladden the sod walls.

I left and walked familiar paths through the dying village.

The ground swelled from the ambient moisture that would soon become an icy kiss. I breathed the scent of the first squall and tasted the cool salt from the coast. I passed the invader's temple which had once been the common dwelling where we gathered to share in merriment or counsel. None stopped me to speak, for that was forbidden. Ever-watchful guards carried ancient weapons of fire and light, but it was their cruelty and barbarism that devastated. Two made a move to halt me, but they let me be when they spied the betrothal necklace and their god's prayer beads. They smirked and spoke vile things in their cursed tongue, not caring if I understood. The foreigners only laughed at other's' pain, and their women had never known joy from their first breath.

That is what became of men with no mothers nor sisters, and no love from their fathers nor brethren.

Installed governors had taken a shine to several young women of our village. The rest of us—whose faces were not as pleasing and whose cunts had known other men—were parceled off to soldiers, lesser sons and brothers. The abomination who was to claim me as if I were a goat reeked of rotten flesh and loose bowels. I pitied the girls who had scarcely a foot in womanhood who had been taken first because they had not known the embrace of a boy and lacked the maturity to fight.

I made my way to the high cliffs facing the sea, following the worn, narrow pass. Far below was where women had long given birth in the tide pools and where my people gave our dead to the tides. From water we come and to water we return. I removed the shell band from around my arm and dropped it. Every child separated from their parents this way.

The rising ocean storm slapped my cheeks until they were ruddy, and my lips froze on my teeth. I let the wind take my cloak, I cut my braid with my contraband blade, and I tore away the vile necklace. My intended surely would presume my death.

The violent squall's fists followed me to the Sabine Caves where I had squirreled away a stocky horse—a creature the foreigners called an old nag and would never miss—and meager supplies. Food could be found in the wilds if one had the wherewithal.

I knew my place in this world.

I was the storm.

CHAPTER TWENTY-ONE
Welcome to Tin Town

A ROLLING STORM THREATENED. RAINDROPS DARKENED the steel rails and the crushed rock between weedy railroad ties.

"The May apples *are* ripe. You have a nose!" Leevi's aging mother, Riva, burst through the wood's edge laden with the dead-ripe, yellow fruit. The ambrosial fragrance danced in the midsummer heat and upon Riva's sticky chin. Earlier in spring, the plant's foul-smelling, beautiful blooms had given it away. Its medicinal properties would be welcome in their pharmacopeia.

"My vovi called these wild jalap." Riva stroked Leevi's lush hair, arranging it to cover the bald spots. "Did I ever tell you, I called you my little jalap when we found you?"

Leevi shrugged one shoulder and updated the harvest location of the plants in her log. "We should transplant some along the route for next year, Momi."

Riva nodded and patted the bursting satchel at her side. "Hmm, wind's pickin' up."

The small hover-cart, laden with hot meal tins, whirred between the abandoned tracks at the border. They'd made the journey together daily, heedless of weather, to deliver sustenance to the town that lay between the wilds and the city proper. Leevi plucked wildflowers from the overgrowth and added them to the daisy chain wreath fashioned from the pickings.

Leevi considered the sentries at stand-by along the border. They'd been programmed to uphold the treaty and law, but not to distinguish physical appearances. Abandonment had been her best protection. Over the line, she was untouchable.

Riva kissed her daughter's troubled forehead and motioned to the flowers. "Don't fret so. Hard times; hard choices."

Leevi tried not to think the worst, though sometimes—when alone—she'd throw stones at the tub where she'd been left until her shoulder ached. Had her birth parents been horrified when she'd been born? She pressed a hand on her chest where her identity badge hung under her clothing. It proved her citizenship but revealed no past or family history apart from her adoptive one. By law, individuals obtained citizen status in infancy and were assigned residency via blood sample. Only limited circumstances allowed for a zone change.

Riva's wrist communicator beeped Morse code.

"Hildy's calving. Popi needs me. You alright alone?"

"Of course." Leevi's voice wavered only a little.

"Mind you watch for snags." Riva inspected the flesh-toned latex covering Leevi's body. "The Purists have been riled lately. Bored of themselves I 'spect."

Balking over the fussing, she turned away from the affection. "Go, Momi."

Riva dropped her hands and backtracked the way they'd come. "Be home for suppin'."

Leevi smoothed a palm over her cheek. She tried to remain inconspicuous and took care not to find trouble or draw unneeded attention. But two night's past, during an impromptu visit with a friend, she had stopped a marauding city-boy from assaulting a Tin Town girl by the path leading to the latrines. He'd pinned his quarry and sat
upon her chest. The girl had been gasping under his weight, trying to

avoid the spittle he delighted in depositing in her ears and eyes. The bastard couldn't have been more than sixteen.

"Hey! Get off!"

"Mind your business, *scabber.*"

Leevi hadn't paid attention to the slur, yanking his hair without hesitation to give the girl a chance to defend herself. He yowled and countered by pulling both of her ankles. She landed on her back and lost her breath. During the scrabble, he'd got the better of her and landed a punch that tore the coating on her cheek. The recovered girl pelted him with rocks and he retreated. Leevi hadn't thought he'd seen through the guise in the dark, yet she couldn't be positive. She shouldn't have been there that late and alone.

She should have told her parents.

Leevi sighed and placed the finished wreath on the old wash tub beside the rails where she'd been left sixteen years prior. Had her birth parents been horrified when they first saw her? She couldn't bear herself sometimes. The disguise protected her and everyone from the wrath of city-folk, but she had to admit it had become a means to hide from herself.

∞

Tin towns were named for the tin-roofed hovels packed in squares of twelve surrounding a meager garden. Residents, the discards from their host city, eked out lives on the fringes. Sentry bots kept townspeople, who were considered criminals by city inhabitants, confined while allowing human free-folk from the wilds and city-dwellers to enter and leave.

Leevi whistled from the town's edge.

"Hey, hey!" The people called, clustering around the hover-cart.

The youngers gathered the sacks of produce and ground grain for the week to cook communally. Frail elders took one of the one-hundred twenty-seven hot meals; they would share with a child ward if they had one. Her family provided rations for the area from their permaculture farm. When the treaty lines with the Peltatu, beings from another world, had been drawn, their land had had a fortunate position in the buffer zone.

While a pepper-haired woman helped distribution, Leevi counted rain-soaked heads. "How's the water purifier, Genevieve?"

"True as the monarch since your brother rebuilt the drive."

"I'll let him know." Leevi pulled several corncob and corn husk toys from her hip-pouch and handed them to the little ones.

Mud caked Genevieve's boots and canvas trousers. "Got the cloth and cobbles ready for your Ma. Folks'll be wanting more tiles and pots from Redclay."

Leevi's family offered trade services among all the tin towns, each having a specialty or service such as textiles, shoe cobbling, or clay pottery and brick. "Might be a hard go, Genevieve. Their solar-kiln has been feisty. We'll ask what they can spare."

Children were thin but energetic, and Leevi jotted down a reminder to discuss a ration increase. As she inspected the crowd, she couldn't help but wonder if she'd ever see another like her or any of the Peltatu. Old-timers, who had seen a Peltatu face-to-face, made up the bulk of the inhabitants of Tin Towns. They'd been banished for "dissonance crimes incompatible with human-first ideals". Sympathizers were all criminals and aliens in Purist's eyes.

She knew little about Peltatu or the war they had brought with them, only that they came not from beyond the Milky Way but through the last Great Rift before it closed. The blue-skinned Peltatu had retreated to the high mountains, deserts, and deep oceans. Humans kept the cities, wilds, and towns. Few people lived feral and free the way her own family did. Strict protocol kept the wilds' numbers down. When the population reached a critical point free-folk were obliged to relocate relatives to Tin Towns. Some said there were Farlands where all folk were free. There were rumors that a coalition was planning to build neutral cities in the sky. A notion, Leevi thought, best left to the fancies of children. The Purists, powerful behind their impenetrable walls, would never allow it.

An abrupt silence in the hubbub caused an uneasy tingle to crawl up Leevi's back to her nape. Her stomach sank, and her pulse quickened.

A cluster of three men and two women from the city led by a teenage boy tromped through the town. Cityfolk rarely came to help: most harassed and turned the unwilling into lurid playthings. The boy pointed at her. Leevi recognized him from the night she'd stopped his assault. The crew, who carried batons, hastened their pace. They pushed and punished people not even in their way for the sake of it.

"*Feke*. They got pain rods." Genevieve shoved Leevi. "Get to the border. Run!"

If she reached the end of city jurisdiction, they could do nothing since urbanites were not permitted in the wilds. The robot sentries would incinerate them the moment a foot crossed the border; they kept the peace everywhere among humans and between Peltatu.

Knocking over several food tins and almost toppling over in her haste, Leevi dashed back to the tracks. She panted uphill, shoes sliding on the slick ground and wet foliage. Villagers tried barring the way, but the Purists had no qualms about concussing and zapping anyone in their path.

Her pursuers caught her twenty feet from safety. A pain rod struck her behind the knee.

They tore her clothes and the latex covering her cadaver-gray skin, kicked, and dragged her body. As Leevi's cheek scraped in the coarse mud, she regretted not hugging her mother that morning.

"I told you! Dirty *skyd!*" The fresh-faced teen pressed his knee into her back. The ubiquitous slur for Peltatus echoed the city's firm, purist platform. More townspeople rushed through the downpour. The children arrived first, throwing stones, and border sentries issued the first warning to the growing mob.

The purists grabbed her black hair, exposing the prominent patches where nothing grew. Leevi yelped. She'd lost her contact lenses, revealing the ruby iris of one Peltatu eye and the half-blue, half-brown human iris of the other.

The cacophony of voices deafened together: *"Let her go—Take it easy you'll get us fried—The bots are watching—Filthy skyd, cut her—Stop!"*

One assailant yanked Leevi's hand hard enough to misalign the joints and issued an order to the sentry. "Ident!"

A needle pricked a blood sample. The sentry beeped and reported:

IDENT: ANALYSIS

. . .

HUMAN
FREE-FOLK CITIZEN; WILDS

. . .

ALERT: PRIORITY ASSAULT
RIGHT OF CITIZENSHIP INVOKED.
AWAITING INPUT

. . .

The bots deactivated the pain rods then stood down. The Tin Town mob took advantage and held the disarmed, shocked purists at bay with sticks, striking them for good measure. Genevieve comforted Leevi, and a townsman gave his shirt. Her mismatched eyes teared and she moaned as she was helped up.

"What is it?" The city-dwellers stared with disgust.

Born a chimera, Leevi had human blood and the combined physical expression from both parents. The hairless Peltatu blue skin combined with the human hue, manifesting as dull gray. The people she had grown up helping knew and didn't recoil. Certainly not the elders who had rubbed shoulders with aliens and lost their homes to their convictions and sympathies. She wondered, though, if Momi and Popi had once been disgusted, too? She was sure they would never admit so.

"She's free-folk, moron. Big mistake asking for an ident," someone said.

A newborn's citizenship chosen by registry location and documented within half an hour of birth was irrefutable. City-folk once used the loophole to steal fresh born babes from Tin Town, until the law protocol at the city-side gates had been amended to "keep the unsavory bloodlines out".

Leevi limped, crossed over the invisible line, and activated her free rights. She stood as straight as her bruised ribs would allow. "Revoke city proper status of assailants." Her red eye accused. "Welcome to Tin Town."

CHAPTER TWENTY-TWO
The Return

THEY'RE HERE. I CAN FEEL IT. *Welcome home.*

The sky answered with a deluge.

Rain—invisible against the pewter and lavender sky—disappeared into the open ocean's hungry ripples. Araia surfaced slowly and whistled out a slow, steady breath, letting the frigid waves cradle her body like sea kelp while she recovered from her dive. She admired her prizes: a green sea urchin and two large oysters. The sea pushed her toward the backside of a rough, protruding rock and she tucked her body into a crevice, using her feet to prop herself up as if on an invisible chair. The urchin, rare now in that part of the coast, she let go. The oysters she shucked with the knife she kept in her braided loincloth belt—she wore nothing else—and ate raw. They tasted of salt and seaweed. She drank collected rainwater from the shells she'd set upon the rocks earlier. A gull alighted. A meal she could make if she hit it with the small bola, but she let it peck the empty oysters.

Araia removed the numerous braids from her black hair and let the sky wash the sea from it. Gusty winds whipped the strands on her face. Her third lid slipped over her eyes to protect them. The shore disappeared from her vision, but the water focused sharp. The coast was not a long swim for her. The setting sun lit the deserted shoreline;

lights from the few houses twinkled. The days were short and there would be little activity. Still, she decided to wait until the waters turned black before she slipped back into the waves and swam with her head above water. Yesterday's eclipse had enhanced the energy of the living and non-living. This chance would not come again soon.

Once on land, Araia picked her way over the barnacled rocks. Though her flat feet were tough, she didn't want to risk an injury. At first, she felt heavy and sluggish. Her well-knuckled, webbed toes gripped strong to slippery stone. Sensitive fingertips allowed her to assess the jags and crags as she climbed.

I knew you'd have to return one day to face your cruelty.

She followed the instinctive pull. With knife in hand, she made her way up to flat land and ambled through the sleeping grasses and trees. Raindrops beaded on the waxy oil protecting her skin. She crossed a deserted road and took cover in the foliage beside a path that led to a weathered gray and white beach house. A man sat on the last step of the sagging porch.

The rain slowed to a mist.

"I've been waiting for weeks," he said, offering her a neat bundle. "I have clothes for you."

She stepped into the porch light's glow and pointed her knife at him. "Betrayer."

When she lowered her head and bared the subtle points of her teeth, he looked away.

Araia hissed fishy breath into his face. He wilted, hung his head, and strained to appear smaller. Her blade point tapped the place where his beard met the hollow under his ear. Though her heart pounded, she'd long dreamed of separating head from neck. His submissive posture stayed her hand.

"I cannot decide if you are stupid or too smart for your own good." She breathed into his ear then sliced his sleeve.

He followed her inside where she found their fifteen-year-old daughter sitting lifeless in a cushioned chair: underweight, hair thinning, ashen skin. Though frail, she looked like Araia—as pale as her mother was dark. The girl's brown, curly hair was not as lush as her father's and had thinned to wisps. A limp hair bow dangled from a few strands.

"Can you help her?" His voice cracked.

"Naima…"

"Her name is Amy."

"Bad enough to steal her from her mother and keep her from the sea, but you took her name, too?" She snarled, remembering the locks that greeted her when she'd come home.

Naima had just turned six. After all those years aground, the sea's call deafened and Araia departed for a half-year jaunt up the coast, seeking prolific Pagu crabs to devour. Ever since her kind had claimed the seas, this had been the way they weaned their young and replenished a mother's reserves. Homecoming should have been a joyous embrace, not nailed shutters and vacant rooms.

Araia lifted the catatonic girl and wept. "She was born Naima. And when she's grown she shall choose her own."

"I tried to protect her. She required a sensible name." He gripped the edge of the mantle.

Araia's nostril flared. "You lie to yourself, *skelp*. You stink of treachery."

"Out there is no way to live, for either of you."

"It is not for you to decide. You could not control me or trust in my return, so you stole our daughter." Araia spat at his feet. "You've kept her from the water too long. I cannot bear to think how you did it."

"She's not like you. She's civ—"

"Civilized?" Araia laughed. "You still breathe. Have I not shown civility? Did you think to tame me as a pet?"

"I loved you, you know this."

Araia pressed her nose to her child's head and drank her scent. "To possess is not to love."

He did not bar her from the door but pleaded. "Please, will you let her come back?"

"I do not own her. I hope you will be long dead if she recovers to wish it. I'll not stand in the way, but nor will I grant long life to a liar and thief. Go back to your cage—your walled city."

Regret and shame kept her blade from his belly.

Araia walked away, back straight, her daughter cradled in her arms. "I shall dream of your begging and revel in it. When the sea breaks upon the shore, I shall know it is your heart's pain."

CHAPTER TWENTY-THREE

The Gardens of Resurrection

I LOST MY HEART.
It's such an odd thing to lose. I never gave a thought to the rhythmic beats or the pulse at my wrists. But then I died. When I awoke to an existence rather than life, I could think of little else except its absence, and my breaths seemed useless things.

I cannot tell how much time has passed since last I felt a thump in my chest, a quickening at the thought of tender kisses, or a rush from fright. My mind still recognizes those abstract things poets ponder and artists render: love, anger, fear, happiness, and despair. Alas, they've grown pale and thin—atrophied without the blood surges.

I recall joy, but I haven't the heart to speak of it.

Long ago, that wry joke would have amused me.

Despair is my numbed companion now that my dog, Alven, lies dead in my lap. It's my fault; my punishment. I made the choices, one into the next, and he suffered for it. Yet, how could I not reach through the compounding days upon unceasing years, grasp for the briefest of moments, and pretend to live again?

∞

For years, I had wandered daily on leisurely walks around the property with Alven, venturing home of an evening for the formal meals my parents demanded. I'd don my best frock and pretend to dine upon food I was incapable of eating. While dutifully contributing to frivolous conversation, I would push bits with a fork around the plate. Immersed in their illusion, my parents would prattle on about wall coverings, dusty books, or the miracles of nutmeg. "You, Father, will agree with me in this", or "Mother, you have had more experience with matters such as these; have you an opinion?" Afterwards, I'd retire to read the *Adventures of Arabella, The Daughter and the Demon* or peruse some other volume. Sometimes I played our Cristofori *pianoforte* or recited poetry like *The Highwayman* for my parents' entertainment.

Many years past, I had negotiated such motions of obedience in exchange for the privilege to roam the grounds unfettered. This entrenched routine suspended suspicion and hid my transgression when I discovered and befriended a young man squatting in the great wood at the south fence beyond the two estate gardens.

The first time I had seen him in the deep quiet of mid-winter, I scrambled away. I did not return for four days and didn't tell my devoted parents who were wary of strangers. The twelve-foot, arm-thick, black iron bars (a mere hand width apart) forbade my passage and contained my bane, The Beast. They could not, however, stifle the exchange of conversation.

My secret had grown hot in my belly and it almost mimicked a fluttering heartbeat. I had become drunk on the rush of that simple, passive deception. By the time I could no longer distract myself from thoughts of the young man and sought him, the wind had bitten the tail of a blizzard and I feared he had gone or froze to death.

To my relief and delight, an inconspicuous fire had glowed orange outside a makeshift shelter formed of pine branches, cedar and snow. I had brought food and comforts, passed them through the bars, thrown a hardened bread loaf at the shelter, and ran away through the heavy snow. The wind, my night accomplice, blew high drifts that covered my tracks.

At first, I'd left offerings like a nocturnal Robin Hood, but on a clear, blue-moon night when the snow-packed ground resisted a warm front, I lingered.

He'd called himself Kirabo. Our relationship found root with each rendezvous and every surreptitious conversation. I had provided supplies that he paid for with stories from the world outside and the trinkets he carved from scraps of hardwood. I came to understand, that a great many years had passed since my resurrection, more than I had ever fathomed or dared to measure. Technologies had advanced far beyond our humble electric lights and Victrola, a fourth war ravaged, and scattered civilian survivors sought safety in the wilds away from the high cities. What wondrous novelty and verve he carried in word, deed, and demeanor!

"You saved my life." Kirabo had told me the day the last of the snows melted, and the muddy ground had softened. His words dripped with the ache of a good-bye.

"You reminded me of mine."

I had gripped the cold bars and pressed my forehead between them until the pressure made my face ache. The metal vibrated and emitted a high-pitched tone, reminding me of my place. None but animals and the inanimate could pass the enchantments. The only way out was through the front gate.

"Come with me, Saira."

For a moment, I had let myself imagine running out to the world and leaving the Beast behind to starve until it withered to bone

But we were tethered by fate. "I cannot."

I'd not noticed that time had slithered away until my parents had come searching for me when I had not appeared for supper. They had caught me in that moment of carelessness. Devilry, how had I let it slip? Not a word had passed their lips as they had pried my fingers from the bars. Had I let myself scream, I might have never stopped.

"Let her go!" Kirabo had gripped my arm despite the barrier blistering us both. My shirt tore, and my hand flaked where his nails had scored when they dragged me from the fence.

He could do nothing.

I was too free and forgotten all they had sacrificed, they had admonished. How could I betray their trust and flirt with disobedience after all my sins? We'd scuffled, and I'd ripped the key from my father's neck. The notion gripped that if I ran fast enough the barrier would hold The Beast and sever the connection. I hungered for an end to my imprisonment, even if the enchantment tore me apart. Annihilation had to be better than perpetual isolation.

The key had *chinked* into place, the rust had ground in the lock while my hands had prickled with the Beast's taint and turned pale. I hadn't meant to awaken it. The transformation took hold, but I continued resolute until Alven's frantic yelps and squealing barks rooted my feet.

My skin numbed. The hot breath of the foul entity that took over my body seared every muscle and drained my flesh of all color. It brought the rush of its vile temper and a ravenous lust for flesh. With a human sacrifice not yet prepared, my parents offered it my dog to quell its rage.

They watched. Solemn. Accusing.

"We do what has to be done," Mother had said, while I was still lucid and before fur had scarcely touched my tongue.

Long after my parents had gone back to the main house, the Beast had slunk away from my body, leaving me alone in my penance.

∞

I have no more tears for the blood-soaked, black fur. The color returned to my hands, the olive tone flushing with warm crimson.

Never had I had so fine a pet until my desperate melancholy encouraged my parents to change their minds on the unnaturalness of bonding with animals and the burden of their fragile, fleeting lives.

"Better the dog than the rats," Father had said to Mother.

I brought every rent piece of Alven's body to the Sleeping Garden, a fitting place to die and be buried. He had often rolled in the mud under the wrought iron arbor where dozens of dormant clematis vines wove in and out of themselves. Birds nested in the dry bramble and vermin dug deep dens. Naked stems bled green when cut, and the dark humus teemed with worms, beetles, and larvae. Much life in the garden slumbered. Foetid decay became the clean scent of rich, loamy soil.

Owls feasted and built their nests in the tallest tree and searched for fat prey hiding in the dry brush and bramble.

Life resurrected from the rot.

I dug a hole, laid in Alven's body, and curled myself upon the mound. Though parted from his limbs, he had drawn his last, pained breaths over his undug grave. I cannot imagine enduring these cursed days companionless.

I broke the handle off the rusted hand spade I'd used to dig, and plunged sharpened metal into my neck. I wanted to suffer just as so many had suffered under the claws of the Beast.

I feared not; I was already dead.

The shiv fell from the wound that never was. I shrieked, tore the ground, and ripped vines until I fell, spent.

"*Ah! The corpse flower blooms. So long has it slept,*" a gravelly voice said. "*Your life is not yours to give.*"

The stench of sweaty hose, Limburger cheese, rotten fish, feces, and the underlying aroma of sweet flowers wafted from the garden's center. The ministrations of thousands of carrion beetles, flesh flies, and creatures attracted to decomposition chorused like summer cicadas.

I ignored them; I lusted for oblivion.

The creature hunkered inches away in a black mantle. Its great muzzle, full of dagger-sharp teeth that shone like crystal, twitched. A thick, purple tongue licked away sticky drool. Its breath warmed my cheek. "*A life bled here; a sacrifice made. Choose a garden as your forebearers did or fate shall.*"

Before its last syllable faded, the creature reeled back and removed its hood to reveal a changed face. Knotted tar-colored hair framed its ashen flesh stretched over protruding bones. The muzzle softened into a feminine chin, coal teeth, and straight nose. Her dark pupil-less eyes bored into me. Her brows lifted. "*Why did you not choose my sister's garden?*"

I didn't know I had chosen until the she-beast spoke it. "This garden lives," I said. "The other is an undead thing shrouded in illusions."

Alven and I had never traipsed within the abutting Rose Garden, where ever-green stems birthed perfect blossoms and unchanging verdant grass carpeted the ground. No flying, crawling or walking creatures lived there. Weeds never passed the borders and no ivy touched the fragrant white rose arbor. He would growl and whimper whenever we passed it. And I, a heartless dead thing, cowered from it and choked down the bile in my throat from its sick, sweet scents.

My parents often strolled in the other garden among the thornless roses. Those flowers might as well have been paper—the pretty printed skin of dead trees

It was there they buried the spent offerings to the Beast. "The atonement of proper burial for the lost souls," Father had explained, "keeps your sin at bay."

The creature considered me then rolled its eyes back until the pale whites looked forward. "*The young man will die. They have brought him, and the Beast will rend him. I cannot alter the agreement that binds you.*"

I lay upon the ground and begged it to take me. "Break my murderous hands and feed me to the choking vines!"

The creature lay upon the ground and pressed its face to the dirt near my own. "*If he gives himself to death in my garden by your hand, your heart can be restored, and the old bond broken. A new bargain may then be struck.*"

I deserved nothing. So many had perished. "I want Kirabo's life back and my parents freed from this wretched place."

"*Then awaken my garden. The young man must submit to his fate. Haggle*

144

wisely when the time comes."

The creature led me to where the man-sized corpse flower had sent out a fat, ghost-white vine with a small bud. "*A token,*" it said and raised a silencing finger to its lips. The bud moved, bulged, and split. A wet, writhing puppy spilled from it—all black save for the white fur which grew where Alven had suffered damage. It stumbled upon over-sized paws and licked at the creature's feet.

"Your companion renewed, but not unchanged. A sacrifice demands a life in return. I cannot yet return yours."

The she-creature shared the truth of The Bargain, the Beast, and my parents.

Liars, both. My parents had summoned it, forged an unforgivable deal, and I became a vessel. *They* controlled it. They had shackled a rabid beast to do their bidding and forced me to murder innocents in payment for the bargain they had made within that unnatural garden.

A fury bloomed where my pulse should have been.

It was my turn to deceive with pleas and supplications.

∞

"Attend to yourself," Mother ordered from the rear porch threshold, pointing to the stone shed where I was wash the gore away. She'd changed to a fresh, pressed evening outfit with a flounce at the bosom and brass skirt pin holding the modern wrap skirt closed.

I don't know how long I had stood just out of the glow of the electric lanterns perched beside the doorway. They had once been gas-powered and hand lit, until their conversion to electric current sometime before the first Great War. Decades later, enormous, inefficient bulbs had given way to tiny ones that flickered as flame once did.

Flickering lies.

An age ago, Mother and Father had taken pride in having the latest in modern innovation. Our first radio had been the tallest in the market with a chrome face and fine lacquer. Every evening, my nose hovered so close to the dial, it fogged and obscured the numbers and dulled the panel lights. The telephone had been a wondrous device, too, and for a time one could call to just hear music. For seven cents we listened to a grand opera and I imagined the voices were singing the tears I couldn't shed and the vibrations on the megaphone were the pulse I couldn't feel. Such a taste it was! But sometime after the second Great War, my parents cut the lines and removed the devices connecting to the outside world.

"Why would you want to carry such ill news with the burden you already bear?"

"It's for the best. You've become melancholy." Mother agreed with Father. "Do not concern yourself with what you cannot have. It will only bring you pain."

They built a housing booth just on the other side of the gate to house necessary communication devices.

I had obeyed.

I was a fool.

In the shed, a fire lit in the small wood stove warmed the cobbled floor and walls but that wasn't its purpose. I stripped, opened the hot door with my bare hand, and tossed my clothing on top. Smoke billowed and embers popped.

"Always burn them," Father had said the first night the Beast had torn into the viscera of a girl, not much younger than I, who smelled of peaches and a grandmother's perfumed kiss. I remembered her still.

I remembered them all.

"No amount of toil will wash the sin away," Mother told me then, while the taste of human was still hot on my breath and the scent of summer fruits wafted from the chunks of hair in my hands, "but nonetheless everything spot clean."

The memories made the hollow burning in my chest deepen.

A log on the fire cracked.

The replacement skirt and blouse left hanging on a hook were modern as far as I guessed, but it didn't matter. The sleeves were always long, and the skirt never rose above the knee. Practical home-woven wool stockings and a ribbon in the hair, Mother claimed, never went out of fashion.

I immersed my frail body into the cold stone trough, the well water turning murky with blood and soil. My muscles did not hold strength after the Beast left me to bear the weight of slaughter. Had I tears I could weep. Had I heart I could mourn.

The lavender soap never lathered but did the job quick and masked the smells of grim reality. As always, I scrubbed the grime from the draining trough with a stiff bristle brush. *Shiff shiff.* The familiar motion, a macabre lullaby, centered my thoughts. *Shiff shiff.*

Could a lie roll off my tongue?

"Let me speak to him one last time," I would say. "What harm can come of it? Give this to me and I promise to never fall to despair and lament my fate. You may have me as I once was."

With silent lips I practiced.

The shed door, swollen from moisture, closed with a firm *wump* and the lock *clanked.*

No!

I slapped the thick, claw marred wood with both palms. The scrubbing brush cracked in two when I beat the door handle with it. Did they know of my deception before it had a chance to burgeon? I could not think of how. Perhaps, Kirabo had proved too much to handle and they did not think it wise to trust me not to aid him.

They would not waste a sacrifice by dispatching him themselves. Patience.

When the fuel ran out at cockcrow, darkness devoured me.

∞

Staff hadn't been employed to attend to the grounds in decades. The last had been after the Third War: Novee, a round-faced maid with an easy laugh and pastel-colored saltwater taffy in her pockets. Mother—disapproving of her affections, refusal to wear livery, and my lofty delight in speaking with her in the three languages she'd begun teaching me—fired Novee within a year.

After that, repairs and inspections had waned further.

The floor at the shed's north corner, where perpetual dampness lurked, stayed mossy. Deep cracks and joints between stones widened in the thaw and freeze. The spike and chain, rusted and brittle, protruding low on the wall gave way with strong yanks. One hundred twenty heavy links and one collar with key lock. I knew a slow count of each link took four minutes.

I pulled up the wobbling cobbles, clawed the wet earth beneath, and widened the exploratory holes dug by rodents. Headfirst, I squeezed my body through using my hands to shove more debris forward, my feet pushing for leverage. Crags snagged my hair and ripped my shirt. My toes poked through holes in my stockings and scraped stone as I twisted, pulling myself up and out. I crawled a few feet then staggered to the Rose Garden where they would have put Kirabo. The interior house lights glowed in the new evening and the faint tones of record music drifted from an open window. Mother and Father preferred not bear witness to kills, though they would soon exit to unlock the shed door.

Hurry!

Alven puppy-yipped, whined, growled, and paced at the corner of the Rose Garden. Old blood, metallic and bitter, assaulted my nose, tickling at the edges of a ravenous hunger. Profuse slaver whetted my appetite. The Beast waited a breath beneath—gnawing, grinding, writhing. I swallowed gritty, frothy saliva laced with salt and bone. The dark mounting presence of my bane terrified and intoxicated, searing and shocking every dead nerve and muscle.

Please, not yet. I had to explain. I had to hold on to tell him…te—

Smells were as words upon markers. The foot trails where my parents trod and the sweet burn of a summoning circle. Alven: sweet newborn and the stink of squirrel droppings. Kirabo: toasted hazelnuts, ash wood, and musk.

Drool dripped from the corner of my mouth and I doubled over from the pull clawing within my gut and vying to control my limbs.

By the time I reached him, color had begun to drain from my nail beds turning them from pink, to violet, to white. Trussed and gagged and tied to the central tree flush with apple blossoms that would never bear fruit, Kirabo sagged with relief.

My legs would not walk. I ambled upon all fours clinging to the tethers of myself that stretched like the seams on a bursting garment.

"Trust." I rasped, my tongue a slug in a pool of sticky sludge. "Run. To dark garden. Follow…" I pointed first to Alven then in the direction where the rotting garden lay. "Give self…give. Say to it: I give! Say!" The words fell away as I grabbed his bonds and tore them with new fangs and razor claws. His bicep tensed under my grip.

He spoke, but I could only understand the thump of his blood, the fear in his sweat, and the anticipation of a soft throat in my jaws. Delight swelled in my belly over the terror contorting his face. I clenched my teeth against a snarl and held the frayed ropes, shaking them under his nose. I touched the ropes to my neck and tapped my wrists together, gesturing to the tree trunk. His voice, a painful tone devoid of meaning, whined in my ears and created starbursts behind my eyes. My fists beat the ground and I repeated the movements until he complied.

Reality blurred.

The hasty knots strained, and the rope fibers grew warm under friction. On my hands and knees, I ripped chunks of bark with my tethered hands and bit my own arm to stay grounded and buy time, but the Beast burst through my husk at last.

I went no place and everyplace; the where mattered not.

Kirabo's agony found my ears.

∞

Dawn arrived with chariots of orange and mauve. Alven snoozed in the crook between my stomach and thighs as I lay curled on the ground. I dropped the fisted hank of hair and a denuded tibia. From a crumbling bird bath choked by dormant Wisteria vines, I rinsed my mouth. When I finished, pink stains marbled the cracked and pitted stone. The humanity within me demanded I heave up the flesh I'd feasted upon, but the sated hunger seduced me to accept and refrain. Temporary surges of life energy left me afire and trembling with satisfaction.

I was a vessel that desired to be filled.

The she-creature waited, her head tilted to one side. Her eyes, now the opaque blue of the dead, neither pitied nor judged. Fat red worms wriggled around her bare, black feet. With haste, I dug a grave and within it placed all that remained of Kirabo: bones and sinew, gristle and hair. The soil drank the blood pools. Maggots and carrion beetles teemed over the remains before the first clod of dirt refilled the hole.

The corpse flower shivered, and the she-creature stroked its vines.

The ground rumbled and quaked!

A shrill keening from the Rose Garden rattled my teeth. The she-creature smiled, threw back her head, and puffed out a long sigh.

"My sister balks, but her contract is not with you. Rules do not prevent vessels from forging a bargain."

The earth tremored. Vines from the Rose Garden curled around outside to no avail. They were not permitted to grow and invade where life reigned.

"What does she want?" I said, the words strange on my tongue which still tasted of death. "What more evil can be done to me?"

"See beyond pain. She is bound as a child is bound to touch what they should not. As you are bound kill yet desire to save what you cannot." The she-creature furrowed her brow as she walked a circle around me. *"The Bargain requires a replacement vessel. Choose or forfeit."*

"I can't. I won't! You tricked me."

She hissed and breathed indignation an inch from my ear. *"No tricks. Truth. The bargain was not of my making."*

"If I refuse? What then?" I balled my fists until the nails left divots in my palms.

"They will steal another. Debts must be paid."

"Will—any—person do?"

"Young or old. Male or female. Ones such as you—neither child nor adult—bend easiest." She spoke the words with careful attention and regarded me with narrowed eyes.

"Do my parents need to be alive at the same time by the terms?"

The she-creature cocked her head listening for a reply only she could hear. *"No."* She stroked my face with hot fingertips. *"I see your mind, clever one. My sister accepts this choice."*

"I didn't—," I began, but the foul thought manifested in my head so clear.

When my parents next crossed the threshold to the Rose Garden, they would stay forever. One would rise and live by day and the other would resurrect by night, but never would they walk together. Each would devour the other upon waking to satisfy the Beast's hunger. My parents had to atone for every murder they forced upon me. I had endured enough.

I dug my own grave in the Sleeping Garden and wrapped myself in dirt and rotting leaves. After all, I was already dead. My cold body shriveled. Each bone turned to dust in the moments my parents screams and wails first pierced the morning riot of birdsong,

Delivering their deaths instead of torment would have been a kindness, but I haven't the heart for mercies.

∞

I came to in the velvet folds of a corpse flower pod, naked and not unchanged. The crisp air raised gooseflesh on my skin, plump and flush with life. I'd been reborn older with only a blush of youth, and my heart pounded in my chest. Oh, how it hurt! The vice of guilt crushed it. Shame stabbed it. Relief gripped it. My throat itched and ached with a double scar where Mother and Father had simultaneously slit my throat with dual knives to seal their pact.

I could not stop the tears nor scarcely draw breath. The she-creature, who no longer reeked of rot but clean humus and new sprouts, embraced me. I buried my face in her neck, clutched her cape in my fists, and bawled into the heat of her body until exhaustion forced me to cease. Alven had grown to full size while waiting patient and loyal, and Kirabo was not born until a few weeks later (by then I'd found some measure of control if not peace).

The roundness of his face had gone and upon his arms from wrist to crook were jagged scars. By the time the Beast had found him, he had given most of himself away and his end had been swift. We hugged as only two who have met a violent death could. Our clasped hands caused a shiver to tickle down my back and awakened flutters that warmed my cheeks.

The Rose Garden tended itself, thereafter. None may enter nor leave it. I do not listen to the screams. I have no regrets, but I take no pleasure in another's misfortunes no matter how deserved.

The Sleeping Garden cycles as it should between the dying and the living. The she-creature welcomes us in all her forms: when her hair was as black new soil in spring; green as sage leaves in summer and fall, or snow white in winter. When we grow old and the end beckons, we will return to the corpse flower to feed it our blood and spent bodies and it will renew us. One for one; new from old.

I understood what my parents couldn't fathom. Sacrifice did not mean innocents had to die.

CHAPTER TWENTY-FOUR

Snow White, Rose Red, and the Key

SNOW PREFERRED A MORE LEISURED amble but pushed to catch up with her sister. The fresh, wooded trail was soft underfoot and slender twigs assaulted them as they passed. "We could stay, Rose. It was not so bad there."

Rose grunted. "Not after you healed all those people in the ER."

Brambles and branches trembled from the hacking wrought by her sister, and Snow clucked her tongue over the carnage.

"What did this sapling do to you?" She smoothed her long fingers over the slender trunk, and the birch shivered upright as the jagged break mended. The leaf litter at her feet shriveled to dust. In a cycle of give and take, she siphoned healing from death's humus, like mushrooms on a damp log.

Snow had saved hundreds at St. Martin's, but at a cost. She'd caused dust mounds in the morgue and quickened the dying of the dark souls. Some fell dead in triage; not all had been patients.

"What you did was reckless."

"A parting gift." Snow made defiant fists at her sides. "Always leave a place better than you found it."

"How many have you healed for nothing in Dunganan?"

"Not for nothing." Her nature sought to gather power only from the evil, dead, and dying. But Snow's perpetual power-high waned outside the city limits, leaving her weak and sickened from the withdrawal.

After placing one hand on the ground and then upon the gnarled oak, Rose sniffed. "That place was rot. All of it."

"Not all of it."

"Oh?" Rose leaned on her walking stick with a smug tilt to her head. "Were you ever short of decay to draw on?"

"You are just sore that you cannot hunt demons in the city." Snow's balance wavered, and she sucked a steady breath. Her mind strained and played tricks sometimes. Gifts cost dearly. Memories came and went. Her world stayed fuzzy around the edges. "You miss that handsome golden bear. Such a fine beast."

"No!" Rose beat a thorn bush to punctuate. "I'm *galled* you got us locked out of the glen. Sixty years!"

Rose's blessings lay in dealing death. Snow understood that the lack of hunting had irked her sister. City life had taken its toll.

She hadn't seen this much zeal from her sister in…oh, she couldn't remember when. Time and memory were incompatible things.

"I am not the one who went gamping after that beady-eyed gnome, sister." She muttered.

"*That* you remember?" Rose grabbed Snow's short, white hair and yanked. "He was a tree dwarf. And *you* lost the key." Her sister's yelp satisfied so well that Rose pulled twice more.

A kick to the shin sent Rose hobbling and Snow threatened to rap her knuckles with a stick. "You've become too human. Are you ever not angry?"

"Look at us! Look at my hands! We're withered and wrinkled. My *muff* has gone gray." Rose kicked a dirt clod. "I told you not to follow. *You* got lost."

"Your hair is the color of starlight, you know. Very fetching. Fie! Flicking a finger at me is not nice!"

"You'd better be right about that key."

"It should glow in the day-moon. We need to get close enough." Snow gazed downward at the dappled crescents of light upon the forest floor. The moon eclipsed the sun inch-by-inch. "It feels like my dream here."

A foul, city-curse burst from Rose. "Dreams are wisps and feelings torment. Remember!"

"I cannot. I try. I do!" Snow bent, lifted a pile of wet leaves, and inhaled. "I swear it smells right. I feel I have been here. I have dreamed this." Mud and debris colored the deep lines of her face.

"Fine. The river's this way." Rose led them left, shoulders sagging with the burden of an eidetic memory hoarding moments and minutiae.

Every life taken and every emotion with it burned forever in mind was Rose's curse. She preferred the empty recall of demon slaying and took care to bring only welcomed mercy or necessary death to mortals.

"We do not need to be young and everlasting again. Forget the glen. Come back to our house and garden and our friends."

"We can't, you demented twit. Do you even—" Rose sighed and dragged her palm across her forehead.

Snow blinked trying to capture the fraying threads of conversation. "Silly. Of course, we can. Let us grow old and fade away. We have lived enough, yes? So many seasons to count by hundreds or thousands."

"You can't remember if you put on underwear this morning." Rose grabbed her sister's hand and dragged her along the deer trail.

Snow peeked under her waistband and muttered dazed, "Oh my."

She sighed and pulled her hand away and headed back, punting rocks and bits of fallen bark. "Home. It is all sharper there."

Rose rubbed her temple. The debacle at the hospital couldn't be undone. Rose crumpled her shoulders inward. "I *need* the glen."

The plea, so unlike Rose, halted Snow's feet; she shivered at a pale memory.

They had followed the White Doe after they helped the creature escape the desperate hunters from their village. That winter had been hard, and they had been the only children to survive the famine and frost. The White Doe led them deep into the Black Wood where trees rivaled the height of giants and where ancient magic gathered away from human expansion. The Spirit of the Glen bestowed upon them their gifts so that they might leave their mortal lives and find favor among the *Awla*—the forest's children. Curses kept the balance within the blessings. Rose had always been the more adventure minded and the role of huntress suited her natural talents, and thus whatever instrument was used to bestow death became infused over time. With enough essence Rose could restore, heal, or enhance life.

Snow held tight to the moment of clarity, but she could already feel it evaporating like fog in an afternoon breeze.

Rose blew air through her quivering lips then pressed her arthritic fingers together. "You don't remember. I killed"—she still wouldn't say the name—"the gnome with my bare hands. I didn't mean to, but that act gave me everlasting life. I don't need the glen to live like you. I'll grow ancient until I'm whispers and dust, but I'll live on." Her voice tremored. "That I could abide, but don't make me watch death take you."

Snow embraced her sister and sensed her part. "I came too, late didn't I?"

They pressed their heads together in comfort.

The wind tousled their hair together in a twirl of blizzard and starlight. In silence, they came apart and walked to the clear, white river where the last of the magical things gathered in a world overtaken by metal and oil. Legends told that in the summers at just the right magic hour a person might witness the river becoming a man and the strange purple flowers (which grew nowhere else) a woman.

The eclipse approached full and the last of the light winked out. Night usurped day.

"Oh, consequences, consequences. We shall pay dearly to return." Snow snapped her knuckles and paced, frenzied. "Which way; which way; this way?"

Rose held fast to her sister, though Snow twisted and struggled to turn around. "You said you dropped it at the three pillars by the river. We haven't got time to chase our tails."

"The key is not here. I *feel* it."

Rose shook her head and moved away with determined strides. She searched the river mud, poking at stones and lifting logs. Muck spilled over her boot tops.

"We'll be punished." Snow bent over to ease the ache in her back. The gnome had been a nasty piece of business, but there were rules against the murder of an *Awla*. "I'm afraid."

"The burden is mine alone. I'll pay the price due. You'll be safe."

"Follow me." From the riverbank, Snow offered her hand. "Please." Not afraid for herself, but for Rose, Snow vowed to be with her through it, no matter the punishment.

The words lingered a long moment before Rose clasped the wizened palm and let her sister take the lead.

"I shall very much miss our garden. I was looking forward to the Wisteria blooms."

"We can sow another. Two, even." Rose squeezed her sister's frail fingers. They chased Snow's cracked memory until their hearts thundered and the sunlight returned sliver by sliver.

Ahead, something glinted in the underbrush.

Tara Lee Davis

CHAPTER TWENTY-FIVE
The Tale of the Seventh Wife

"I'M CLEARLY DOING SOMETHING WRONG." The canvas sack muffled a woman's voice. "Why else would my betrothed toss me in a bag over a horse's rump. Did my father not promise me to you? Did you not witness my vow to stay 'til your last breath?"

There came no answer but the clop of hooves. Surely, the man with the long beard searched for every ditch and divot to drive the animal over.

"An affront, sir! An indignity. You wish a whining, wailing bride? You shall have it!"

And she keened in such a pitch that the beast balked, and the horseflies fell down dead.

The bells and buckles on his coat *chingled*. The sack he pitched and, with his bejeweled blade rent a hasty slit. The squall ceased the moment fresh air touched her lips.

"Enough!" His fingers he wound in her brown curls and his knife he pressed to her throat.

Oh, how she squinted, coughed, and gagged! "Dispatch me quick for I cannot endure the slow death from your fetid breath." She wondered how he did reek so, yet his hair he kept braided slick and banded with gold.

He did threaten to relieve her of her hands and she did admonish that a handless wife could not cook. He did threaten to remove her feet and she did scoff that a footless wife could not clean. He did threaten to remove her tongue and she did shrug most slyly.

"Walk, woman." Her wrists he bound and tethered the leashing rope to the ornate saddle.

"Adalia, if you please. I will wish to answer nature's necessity at noon, four, and at eve's sup."

From that moment, she complained not—even when pebbles stuck between toes and soles wore paper thin—but only listened to the melodies of the mockingbird that followed.

By and by, when journey's end found his home, she gave to him the rope undone (for she had a fancy for unknotting and his were but a child's), and there stood obedient. Flex his bulk and sneer did he before he offered to her a heavy, golden key ring. Among the seven jeweled keys hung one of somber iron bowed with crimson silk.

"The house be yourn to roam. Any room but the one beyond the iron door." He tapped the beribboned key with his knife. "Enter—"

"—Aye, aye. Enter and die." A slitting motion she pantomimed across her own throat with her thumb. Nary a worry line crept upon her brow.

The sneer again crossed his hairy face. "You may yet live."

"May it be, for I have promises."

"I grant a year and a day's mourning." Rubbed he a distended belly and stretched. "Your brother should digest by then."

A mournful melody the mockingbird trilled for the sorrow Adalia dared not reveal. Such times as these had not a place for a tear.

From first night to sennight to fortnight Adalia did ingratiate herself. The fire she kept stoked, the chores she dutifully completed, and for her pleasure fashioned a perch by the dining hall for the wee bird. Its arias warmed the rooms and brightened her spirits.

The birdsong came to her as words and revealed terrible secrets.

The man she came to call Bluebeard (for the sapphire rings he liked to weave within the whiskers) did taunt her every morn: "I take my leave. Enter the forbidden room and I shall feast upon your flesh more heartily than I did the boy."

Stoic as cold stone and with the honor of her promise to ne'er utter a complaint, Adalia served to him his courses, repaired his shoes, and polished his noisy coat.

She possessed no desire to open the door to the forbidden room, for the little bird had told her that six curious brides had met a grisly fate within. Their blood blackened the floors and their bones hung as trophies. At times, Bluebeard appeared in the afternoon suspicious and yet only found vexations when he found her embroidering or whistling. As fortnights turned to a half-year, each evening he brought to her gifts of dresses and gems.

Quoth he every eve, "You may yet live."

The first gowns she accepted for he had let her bring nothing, but then did scold him. "I have already seven frocks. One neck and ten fingers I own. What use are more silks and baubles?"

Bluebeard gifted to her an enchanted, golden cage for the bird that would force it to sing whenever she did desire. "What need have I to capture what gives me freely?"

Her life he granted one day to the next, and his trust, it grew 'til he had quite forgot his part in the gruesome feast.

On the eve before the last mourning day (when the brandywine was poured), Adalia braided for her betrothed his long beard. Before the logs had gone to orange coal and his eyes closed contented, she did puncture his throat with the dagger pins holding her hair.

Oh, how the fresh blood splattered! The spray did soak the mockingbird and, at once, it transformed into Adalia's murdered brother. For the trouble of being eaten and for his essence having found sanctuary in feathers, his hair thereafter remained a dusky, downy gray.

Together they did bury the slain brides' bones and sent their spirits to rest. Whispering willows and mauve blossoms forever sprang from the barrows. The pair took the house as their own, for they had no home left to return to. Adalia set Bluebeard's severed head into the bewitched cage to keep ever after upon death's door and never to cross over.

Every night she did whisper, "You may not live, but you may watch."

CHAPTER TWENTY-SIX
The Daughter and the Demon

ONCE, IN A LAND WHERE sorcery might tame a dragon and a mountain might speak to a mortal, a baby girl was born to a poor young woman. The infant took breath on the third hour, on the third week day, of the third month, in the third ruling year of the new king. At once, the wizened recognized the marks of destiny and they each took their turn at the King's ear. The great oracles, from the four points of the world, had foretold of such a child who was destined to sit upon the throne and bring fortune to the kingdom.

All took this to mean the pauper would wed the crown prince—a boy who had seen three seasons.

The King's mood grew as dark as the berries on the nightshade trees that grew in the Blackwood Forest. Not a stranger to nefarious plots, he had dispatched the previous ruler with the aid of a usurper second queen who had won her place through deceit. The King's plans for his son did not include betrothal to a gutter rat.

Full of ill intention, in the garb of the royal guard, he slipped into the mother's hovel and deepened her slumber with the vapors from the roots of the Indigo Valerian. The babe, whose flush of black hair shone almost blue even in the night, did not stir. The King had in mind to fill the cradle with blood and place blame upon the woman

163

for the vile deed. Oh, fortune's bewitchment! The blade shattered in its sheath the moment the king's hand clasped the hilt. A barrel-drowning he tried next, but the bindings and staves burst apart. The hearth fire snuffed and turned cold the instant he tossed her into it. Bludgeons turned to dust and ropes would not tighten. Vexation! Determined to be rid of the babe, he stuffed her into a basket, packed it with rocks, bound it with twine, and threw it into the cold White River.

With pomp and circumstance the next morning, he visited the hovel in the guise of friendship (by then all knew of the prophecy and expected the king would groom the child for a life of royalty). He accused the dazed and distraught mother—who had barely shaken the induced sleep from her eyes—of murder of the most egregious kind. None heard from her again, nor would any befoul their tongues with her name.

But murder had not been done.

The lucky basket had been woven from whettle reeds which held within them tiny chambers of air and possessed a property of swelling watertight (a true buoyancy even under heavy weight). For three nights, the babe dozed in the cradle of the river. She did not cry nor wake under the spell of the river's lullabies. The rapids quieted, and the current brought the bundle to the home of the Millers who had wept their sadness to the waters. They had not been blessed with children. With joy at their fortune, they promised the river that the babe would find comfort and love in their family.

As it was and ever shall be, years pass, deeds fade, and children grow.

There came a day when fate decided the His Majesty's carriage should throw a wheel and lose a horse. The King and his entourage found refuge at the mill for the night. The Millers thought it was their greatest honor that royalty should end up at their front door (their lands were not proximate to the castle and leagues thinned the rumors of misdeeds)

They made accommodations and moved out of the tidy main cottage to the mill house so that His Majesty might repose in privacy. The King took interest in their daughter whom they called Thala—a name which meant three and thistle in the old tongue (for when they found her she'd had three thistle seeds stuck in her hair).

"Loyal subjects, I notice your tresses are as fair as the hay upon the farm hills and your daughter's is black as coal pitch."

"Your Highness, it is as you say. Fate smiled upon us eighteen years ago and the river brought us the child we longed for," Mother said, with a hand to her breast and tears in her eyes.

"We presumed dark times befell her parents as it has for so many, and we raised her as our own." Father spoke with pride and a quiver in his voice. He patted Thala's face and smoothed down her hair that she always kept short for a working life. "A finer young woman you'll never meet."

Thala curtsied as her mother taught her though she was in soiled trousers. She put a hand to her throat to draw courage from the thistle necklace her parents had made from the lucky seeds. "T'was a fortuitous day, Majesty."

The King hid the growing frustration rumbling within. He thought to dispatch them all there and leave their bones to crush beneath the great grind stones, but a bewitching in the air would not allow him to put his hand to sword against Thala. Whenever he drew near the hilt his arm locked and would not draw. He had a mind to kill her parents but thought leverage a better tool.

It was then that he knew that Thala was the accursed babe he'd hope to lose in the White River. The King paced, turned upon his heel, sat down at the table, and called for a parchment and quill.

"Trustworthy and true?"

"None more, Sire."

The Millers had no reason to learn to read for they had all they needed in mind. Thala—as was her nature—was ever curious about the script. She could not read well, but kept her eyes averted lest she glean what she was not invited to see. The King rolled and bound the parchment with the royal seal and handed it to the Miller's daughter. He bid her to deliver it straight away to the castle by her own hand, escorted by his most trusted guard.

"It is a matter most urgent," said he. "I have a mind to reward your family, but a test of loyalty I require. Do not tarry. Remember, I shall be here waiting." For amusements, the King had often given such tests (many fool's errands and one-way journeys). He once promised a poor fellow a flagon full of jewels to find a needle in a haystack or fail and be chum for the moat avank. There were none who would refuse, though they knew success was not theirs to hold.

Thala gave her word and set off on the back of a donkey.

∞

Thala had led a sheltered, quiet life helping her parents and making herself useful in the nearby villages. She had a knack for fixing and had many times been called to mend one thing or another. When the old mill groaned and got its gears stuck, she could find the problem faster than her mother. Contentment had been her shelter and little tragedy beyond those of the normal course of living had ever darkened her spirits. She did not know the exact way to the castle, yet she felt disquieted when they turned away from the river which had always been a confident voice that had guided her since her childhood.

"Sir, I hope you will excuse me, but shouldn't we follow the river?" asked she, and her escort replied that the journey was best overland and not by the water's whims.

The guard led them deep down the most dangerous roads away from the castle towards the southern docks where the underhanded and devious plied their business and where even the pirates preferred not to lay anchor. The King had instructed him to sabotage their travels with all due cunning and sell the miller's daughter to the lowest bidder—though he would have favored her heart wrested from her chest, enchantments would not allow it.

"Find the merchant with the blackest reputation, farthest port, and the most questionable ship. If you can't sell the wretch, pay for her passage," said he.

If the guard found failure, the King had yet another plan in motion.

When they set camp, Thala stayed huddled by the donkey for warmth. The guard ate thrice the ration Thala's mother had packed and advised against any fire. The wind raised the hairs at her nape, whispered warnings from the river, and would not let her sleep nor rest. Trust not, the zephyr advised.

The next morning Thala could not move her feet to go forth—rooted to the spot as if great weights were put into her soles. The guard grabbed her by the arm and pulled her fruitlessly.

"I do not think the ways of the world wish me to go that way. My shoes are fixed!" She didn't know why or whence, but when shoes dared not travel forth, a body should listen.

The guard—thinking himself clever—untied her laces and tossed her over his shoulder. "We go."

They had not gone five strides when the root of a tree twisted up from the ground and tripped them down a steep embankment. Thala's traveling dress got caught up in a jagged rock that slowed her fall and tangled in thick bramble until it was flung over her head. Thankfully, she had the wherewithal to wear her best bloomers. The donkey brayed in dismay as Thala climbed back up with the help of rock and root which were always right where she needed them.

"Old Fellow," she told the donkey, for that was his name, "I fear he means to do me harm."

The guard's curses and vile promises of what he would do when he found her echoed far below. His voice soon faded further and further away. Thala didn't move for quite some time unsure where to go until she decided to consult her shoes. Wherever they led her to walk, that was the way to go.

She had always been followed by moirai, kismet, and strange

happy accidents that kept her from calamity. She didn't think the shoes were bewitched, but merely that events sometimes occurred in a satisfactory way. An old log could float on by if she were tipped from a boat, her clothing might snag to keep her from a hole, or a chickadee might startle her away from a path.

She walked and rode Old Fellow for a full day and night until a storm raged, and she came upon a well-worn inn with a red door in the middle of the night.

"Please, madam. I am the miller's daughter and I have been entrusted with a task from the King. I require shelter for the night though I cannot pay."

"And the Queen loves my pies." The petite red-haired woman— half as tall as the door—scoffed. "This is no place for you, this den be for robbers and thieves. On your way, child."

The innkeeper pushed the heavy door to close it, but donkey had set its head and hoof between and brayed for dinner and shelter. Thala begged as she shivered in the downpour. "I beg you. I fear I will catch my death in another moment. I daren't go another step." Her teeth chattered so loud it sounded like a pickaxe on stone.

"The lot come often. Can't promise safety and I'll not turn them out. Pay's too handsome when them's lofty from a good haul."

"I can't explain it, madam. I shall be safe here. I know it as I know the rightness of it all."

And with the last word she collapsed.

The innkeeper had just pulled Thala to warm her in the fire when the door flung open. A rabble of seven thieves burst in ravenous with an unquenchable thirst and high on the spoils of plunder.

"Red!" They called and whistled for the innkeeper. "Break a cask and fill the tables!"

Coin purses clinked, weapons clanked, and chests clunked as they were set upon the long dining tables. They reeked of road, horses, and sweat. Red admonished them after leaping upon a chair and clanging on a pan to get their attention.

"Your rank offends my pots and hounds! Off with you."

The men and women, rough and rowdy, did as told. One did not argue with a fire pixie under her roof. The ruffians bellowed and clambered over themselves to get to the hot springs baths below the inn first, but their attentions were waylaid.

"'ere now, what's this? A new pet?" The tallest of the women, Brigit, nodded to the waterlogged Thala who had not stirred yet despite the noise. "Not like you to take in gutter rats, Red."

"Feh! Fell inside my door. Tried to roll her out but the thing just rolled the other way. Got my floor all wet, too."

"What's a Little Bit like that doing this deep, eh?" A man with a plaited beard bent low and sniffed at Thala. "She smells like bread."

"Slave you reckon?" Brigit asked no one in particular. "The mines are near."

Another knelt. "Naw. Too clean. Ain't got no chains nor brands. New capture from the docks, yeah?"

Red jumped down from the chair and began to prepare for service. "Says she's on a mission from the king."

The seven laughed. "Is she now?"

They chuckled and guffawed and disappeared for a time below. When all was quiet again—save for the muffled merriment in the bowels of the inn—Thala awoke bleary and trembling under her wet clothes.

"I beg your pardon!"

Red snorted a reply and pulled the bellows and opened the flue chain to get the coals in the great hearth to awaken, but the deep hued fire would not rise higher than an inch. "Stubborn y'are." Red chided and scolded the flames more.

"I think your fire is angry. Look how crimson it is." Thala, always curious, bent close. The flames curled into shapes that appeared at times to be a cheeky tongue sticking from lips or a hand with a rather rude presentation of fingers. "Oh, my! No need for such language, friend."

Thala cocked an ear towards the hearth listening to the creaks and grinds as Red worked it for a while. "I hear the problem. I can fix it, madam. I've a knack for such things. If you would be so kind as to ask your fire to cool the hearth then move to the side?"

Red glanced askance at her sodden guest. There were few strangers who ever addressed or noticed the oddities of the flames much less knew its nature. Fewer still who would recognize the keeper, a fire pixie, with such confidence. "You heard 'er; move over."

The fire wrapped itself up and took away the glow of the coals and the heat from the metal grate. It crackled its way to a small birdcage-shaped ember keeper where it chose the form of a pouting toad.

Thala rummaged through her pack for her simple tools, hopped into the hearth, and set herself to addressing the complaint. A half-disconnected flue chain was the main problem, but there were also loose screws and wobbling workings. Thala asked only for a way to get to the roof and scampered up in her bloomers. By the time she was done and had skirts on again, she was blackened by soot hand to foot. All the while, the room had filled with better smelling criminals and a well spread table.

"There you are, my friend," Thala told the flames that had formed into a snail with curious eye stalks. She laid a trail of kindling back to the hearth's center as if the fluffs and bits were a royal carpet. The fire crept and burst into a wall of bright orange and yellow sparks.

"Fancy that. I haven't seen Ethne that spry in quite a while." Red nodded her approval. "Not so useless as I thought." It was not clear if it was Thala or the fire she was addressing.

"Now, she looks like a mine rat!" one of the rabble said after a long draught of grogue.

"Oh, I am a mess to be sure." Thala approached the biggest man who sat alone at a table tinkering with three broken music boxes. She smiled politely and held out her hand. "I can fix that, if you please. I've a way with workings and mechs. You have a farmer's strong hands and those bits need a light touch."

Startled, he handed it to her, for she had not recoiled from his hunkering appearance, scars upon his face, or cauliflower ears. None but his three daughters ever looked at him that way—as if his ugliness was of no consequence. Thala deftly fixed the three boxes with the odds and ends she was always squirreling away with her tools. One never knew when they would need a little coiled spring, lens, a screw, or a little gear. Soon she was overrun with requests to repair little trinkets and baubles. Red even let her sit at the table to eat unwashed—save her hands.

"Why ain't you afraid, girl. We could kill you as easily as look."

Thala, bent over a necklace chain and worried over a stubborn link. "I suppose that is true for villains. Yet, such vile persons would have slain me the first they saw me slumbered. Or woke me, done unspeakable things, then dispatched me. Or, perhaps, sold me when they were done. I see professionals of looting, robbery, and thievery, but not a villain among you."

This amused them and set them singing crass ditties to make the naive girl blush, but she did not.

Thala trusted the bewitchments in her life and was assured that they would not send her to a den of morally corrupt curs. The seven had not always been plunderers. Once they had been a scribe, a merchant, a farmer, a blacksmith, a bread maker, a tailor, and a tutor.

When Thala passed out by the fire—which sent grateful little white smoke birds to sit in her hair—they began to rummage through the few things she carried (they were thieves after all) and found the sealed letter in the satchel. They pried it open with the help of pot and steam. Even the least learned among them could read, for there were many documents that were worth a horse's weight in coin.

"That Little Bit got herself in a fine mess with that Usurper." Brigit huffed. "Listen to this...

'My Queen,

Misfortune has delayed me and, yet, providence has allowed this opportunity to free ourselves from the shadows of prophecy. If this wretch should reach the castle doors have her put to this sentence: set her head in an iron mask, and chain her to the deepest dungeon. Keep the Prince away from this business at all costs and speak not of it to anyone.

By order of the King.*"*

Red stoked the yellow and blue fire and tossed a blanket over the deeply slumbering Thala. "This girl ain't more than twenty. What could she have done to deserve that?"

Most of them had had families of their own once or had them still.

"I tell you, the False King needs no reasons to send a body on a wild goose's tail."

The man with the plaited beard stroked it thoughtfully while plotting with his mates. He had been a scribe and had put his skills to much good use for forgery. He instructed the others to remove the royal seal without blemish from the scroll and set about writing another after studying the King's hand. It read:

"My Queen,

Misfortune has delayed me and, yet providence has allowed this opportunity to right a wrong. It is my hope that this young woman should reach the castle doors and be greeted as royalty. Betroth her at once to the Prince, have a feast in her honor, and escort her to sit upon the throne as a reward for a great deed she has done for me. Do not question all that I bid.

By order of the King."

All agreed that the counterfeit looked more sovereign. They sealed it and slipped it back into Thala's satchel.

The smoke birds flittered around the miller's daughter, dissipating at first light. The robbers and Red sent Thala on her way in the right direction with travel-worthy trousers, boots, and a wool cloak with a beaver-fur hood. The old mule was curried, saddled, and packed with supplies.

"Be well and wise," said all.

"Fortune smile on you," replied she.

∞

The castle gates came into view the morning of the third day and Thala found herself glad for the journey's end. The royal seal granted entry and guards led her to a grand chamber whereupon the Queen received her.

"Your Highness, I am the miller's daughter. I bear a message from the His Majesty, the King." Thala delivered the letter with the lowest curtsy she could manage without toppling upon her nose.

The Queen, dressed in aubergine silk, white ermine fur, and a hoard of jewels, knitted her brows together. Her fists crushed the edges of the parchment. She did not know what game her husband was playing or what drink befuddled his senses, but such foolishness failed to amuse.

"What makes a common doxy like you think she is worthy to marry the Prince?"

Dumbstruck, Thala teetered and fell upon her knees. "Oh! Majesty, ye shall know the truth that none is more unworthy than I."

Pleased with the obeisance, the Queen rose, aimed her nose high, and glided across the marbled floor towards the throne room. "Come."

It was known by those closest to the castle that Her Majesty was fond of separating bodies from heads. The ax—it was said—was the kindness among what other whims might take her fancy.

Thala did not know what to do when the Queen motioned to the great gilded throne (beset with an uncountable number of jewels and precious stones) and commanded that she sit upon it. Her Majesty appeared to offer courtesy and, yet, Thala felt a great unease with the way the noble-born gaze bored through her as if she were a boil upon the world. The company of thieves and plunderers had been the finer party a thousandfold.

"Sit upon the throne as your King demands or pay the penalty for disobedience."

The Queen studied all with a steeled expression. When Thala sat with half her bottom perched on the throne afraid to sit back in comfort, the Queen summoned her ladies-in-waiting. "What the King demands, the King shall have. My ladies shall make your disagreeable countenance less offensive to me. Only then shall you meet the Prince and the conditions of your betrothal discussed."

Thala's mouth bobbed open and closed. Her heart-of-hearts did not extend to thoughts of sovereign matrimony, least of all to a stranger. Although destiny would not allow harm to befall her, she did not think such providence extended to her parents.

The tangles of fate tightened and choked more than the fitted bodice of the blue damask gown Thala had been obliged to wear during a most uncomfortable, indulgent dinner. The Prince entered the dining hall late and breathless with anticipation (wagging tongues had reached his ears), forgetting all formality and greetings.

"Ah! Osric, my son. Had you luck with the falcons?"

"Mother, yes. Fine...sport." Prince Osric bowed his head though his eyes kept dancing aside at Thala, who did not know whether she should bow her head into the silver bowl or squeeze out from the heavy chair to genuflect. Without the river in her ear she felt adrift.

"Come meet your betrothed," the Queen cooed and waved her bejeweled fingers. The enthusiastic expression that caused the Prince's cheeks to flush did not bring favor to his mother. This did cause the darkness of her thoughts to wind themselves into a cunning plan to thwart prophecy. For surely, she thought, the letter had been bewitched or cursed even though her inspection had not revealed any charms. The King's script appeared genuine, but she knew the ways of magic (and wrought binding and barrier spells of her own).

The protections surrounding the girl were ancient, powerful things.

"As your father commands, this will be done—after a test of her worthiness. After all, a transformation from sow to a princess cannot be undertaken without proper scrutiny of honor and loyalty."

"Lady…" Osric bowed and did his lordly best to bring ease and chase Thala's melancholies away. The servants had often noted amongst themselves (for they fancied their heads upon their necks) how unfortunate parentage had not yet darkened the young prince's gentle heart and even temperament.

When alone (save for the chaperones) strolling the grounds, Thala found Osric to be of true mind and expressed her desire—with all due compunction, deference, and reverence—not to wed His Royal Highness.

"Who doesn't want to marry a prince," asked he with a light laugh.

Not wanting tread into treason, she next inquired what it was the Prince would wish for if there were no bounds to his wants? He'd then taken her to far gates flanked by towers that loomed so high a giant need not bend to look through the windows. When he raised his hand to the iron, thick roses sprang up with dagger thorns to bar him. They snagged his sleeve and their odious scent tightened their throats and teared their eyes.

"Much I have, Lady, and yearn for none more than this."

"I am but a miller's daughter, but I would seek a way to free the Prince if the ways came across my path."

"A thousand wise men could not." Osric offered his arm. "Come, let us speak of merrier things."

The next morning, before the sun had yet to kiss the horizon and while the infatuated Prince slept, the Queen summoned Thala and set her to task.

"It would not do to wed a pauper to my son without first assessing her mettle. It is decreed in the kingdom's laws that whomsoever comes from the low born shall fetch from the Farlands three golden hairs from the head of the Night Demon. Refusal and failure shall come from the hides of your family." The Queen hoped to be rid of the irksome girl once and for all, for the Farlands were harsh and the Demon forever ravenous for human flesh.

Thala straightened her back and curtsied. "As commanded. Though I am a mere miller's daughter, I am not afraid."

∞

Thala, in the clothes she arrived in, journeyed north with Old Fellow. The wayroad that led to the Farlands passed through many towns. For the most part, Thala ignored these until the supplies dwindled. She arrived at a large town with crumbling walls late one evening, weary and quite peckish. The watchman at the gates peeked down from above.

"Who goes forth and what be yer knowin'?"

"I am the miller's daughter. I know the knack of things."

"That so? Pray, why does our fountain that once sprung wine lie dry and gives nary a drip o' water?"

She had to concede that she did not know the workings of magical fountains but offered to fix the gate lock and the watchman's lantern. For this, he provided straw to sleep and a ration of bread and cheese for her travels. The next morning, she thanked him.

"I know not how, but I have a mind to find your answer, my friend. Upon my return I shall hope to have it."

Many days farther on, when her belly growled, and her lips cracked with thirst, she approached a sprawling town with gutted roads relieved of their bricks.

"Ho! Who comes forth and what do y'know?"

"I am the miller's daughter. I know the knack of things."

"Hah! Then answer this: Why does our town tree that once bore gold and silver apples lay barren with not a leaf?"

Thala had to admit that she did not know the ways of enchanted trees, but she could remedy the watchman's stove so that it would not pour soot in his quarters and could mend the spyglass mounted upon the gates. For this, the he offered a warm corner to sleep, water for her canteen, and barrel biscuits for her travels. The next morning, she thanked him.

"I know not how, but I have a mind to find your answer, my friend. Upon my return I shall hope to have it."

By and by, when the third month met its end and Old Fellow's nose drooped as Thala led him onward, they came to the Amaranthine River where it was said the drowned did not sleep nor stay dead. A ferry waited at an old, gray dock overgrown with weeds and moss.

The ferryman, holding out a water-pruned hand, shifted his weight on one wood and metal leg. "Who comes? What is your payment?"

"I am the miller's daughter. I beg forgiveness. I've nothing, sir."

"Feh. What then shall we do?"

"You could tell me your troubles while I fix your leg so that it does not grate and squeal so. I've a knack for such things."

The ferryman grunted and allowed her to proceed. "Always I must row back and forth, shore to shore, never a reprieve, and never free. Tell me why this burden binds me?"

Thala had to admit once more that she did not know the ways of bewitchments. However, pleased with the trade, the ferryman took her to the Farland shore and gave her this warning: "All men who come ne'er return. But you are not a man, so heed these words and dare not seek the Night Demon. That is madness and death. Find instead its mother. Wily and wise is she. Pay no attention to her gruff ways; her heart is the only light that dares shine in the Farlands."

The miller's daughter thanked him for his sound advice.

"I know not how, but I have a mind to find your answer, my friend. Upon my return I shall hope to have it."

As it happened, Thala found her way, indeed, to the only light that shone in the night. She thought the Farlands would be a barren white-hot desert or endless swaths of naked, cinereous rock. Instead, she found herself engulfed by the tallest grasses waving in the wind like ripples upon water. Golds, silvers, lavenders, and pinks swayed.

The thatch-roof cottage had a thin stream of smoke coming

from its chimney and its thick cob walls shone a brilliant, fresh white. An old woman with neat, long gray braids rocked while she carded wool tufts. The two stared, surprised to see the state of the other. Thala, grimy and road weary, and the old woman clean and not the vision of a demon's dam.

"Away with you! I do not want your guts defiling my stoop! And they will if my son finds you about. Shoo!"

"Please, madam! I am the miller's daughter and I've been sent by the Queen to fetch three golden hairs from the Night Demon of the Farlands. My parents will suffer my failure." Thala blubbered, pleaded, and rested her forehead to the old woman's boots.

"Ash and gas. Get up girl. You're soiling my apron." The woman sniffed and wrinkled her nose.

"Your odor might be mask enough. Are you a human or an ass? I can't tell. Why should I help you?"

"Madam, I say that I cannot compel you to do anything. But without those hairs I am lost. I could trade? Have you anything with mechs for repair? I have a knack for things."

"Hrmph. There're no trinkets here, child. But I'll help if not for more than a change from the daily rot." She led the way inside and began to prepare a transformation potion for the purposes of hiding Thala.

"I have heard you are wise. If I may, I have three questions."

"Questions or hairs of gold? Which'll it be? You'll not have your wants so easy."

From the depths from which Thala did not know she had, she let forth a tirade of how not easy her current course had been. Despite the gift of luck (or curse of fate) the days grew ever more suffocating. She missed home. She missed the White River.

"Ah, so the supplicant has a voice after all. Try rougher words the next time you find it."

"Take this. I shall buy the answers." Thala dropped her thistle-seed necklace upon the table and stared defiant.

The demon mother's eyes went round. "You would give this?"

Thala blew her nose into a rag. "I've nothing else."

"Do you not know what these are?"

"Thistles?"

"Oh, fortune's folly, these are ensorcells. It is said that when the moon's first smile alighted upon the first flower it bewitched the seeds. They were once spread through the world. No mortal alive has ever seen one and I never thought to see one again." The old woman's eyes teared. "With ensorcells I could craft a potion that would quell my son's hunger and ease the burdens of his curse, though his is too powerful a magic to undo. You can call me, Gertha, and you shall have your answers."

Thala told her of the fountain, the tree, and the ferryman. "Odd questions, true, but none my son cannot best."

The old woman first planted one seed in a teacup and whispered a wish to it before finishing her preparations to turn Thala into a cockroach.

"Oh, calm yourself. What could be safer? You can't be crushed so easy and can skitter anywhere," said she when Thala ran around and around in panicked circles. "Just you listen. You'll not get a second chance." She placed Thala in the teacup (with the first sprout already peeking from the soil) just as the Night Demon of the Farlands burst through the doors.

He stank of corpses and sulfur and his hairs did not look golden beneath the gory mud. He rubbed his head on the cottage beams—for a headache always plagued where his knobby horns grew—before crumpling in front of the fire.

"I smell...human..." He growled and made to rise again.

"Oy, that is you tracking in innards and brain on my floors! How many times do I have to tell you to wash off the man-flesh first? Go to sleep and don't be a pester."

Gertha waited until deep, slow snores shook the crockery then plucked one hair.

"Ach! What was that!" He bellowed and rubbed his eyes.

"Nothing more than a bad dream. You were asking a question."

When he inquired what it might be, Gertha told him of the fountain that no longer gave forth wine.

"Easy that. A toad's stuck in them works. Remove it and the wine it is flowing again."

Back asleep the demon's snorting caused the dust from the roof to sprinkle down. Gertha yanked another hair.

"Arrgh! What pains me!"

"Shh, my boy. Another dream, is all. Such a strange question you asked."

She told him of a wondrous tree that grew silver and gold apples that no longer could sprout even a leaf.

"Strange these dreams is. Not hard, Mutter, not hard. Mice is always at the roots of enchanted trees. Remove them before it withers and fruits there'll be."

The demon yawned and dropped off to slumber a third time. When his snores rattled the windows, Gertha plucked the last hair.

"Ai! Bones and blood! What dream plagues?!"

Gertha patted his head and shushed. "Odd indeed, my darling."

She told him of the ferryman and his fate.

"Foolish is he. The oar need be put in other hands. He be free, and they be not. Hoy!"

She agreed with her son and fed him a sleeping draught so that his aches would bother him no more. He took this in one gulp and would not stir a nose until daybreak—time enough for Thala's disguise to wear off and for the ensorcell to grow a thistle-like head. The flower would bring forth more seeds to plant though none would be as powerful as the first.

Gertha gave over the three hairs and returned Thala's necklace. "These two are priceless. Plant them and speak a wish to each and they will grant it. Such old magic would diminish if I were to succumb to greed. You and I have all we need, child. Go and remember all you have heard."

"I am called, Thala," said she.

"Good journey then, Thala."

∞

Swift feet bore Thala to the ferryman—who was gobsmoggled to rest eyes upon her—just as the dawn sky turned the Amaranthine River a dusky rose. "Oy! Miller's daughter! I thought to leave at first light, and there you be flesh still stuck to your bones. There's a change about you, too."

"Indeed, sir, if crawling about on six legs doesn't change one's marrow I don't know what!"

As he drew the long oar Thala shared the answer to his plight. "The next time one comes to be ferried to the Farlands, give them the oar and be freed."

The ferryman shook his head. "There it is! Never could I put another to bear. Here I row evermore."

Thala pondered this and the fickleness of kismet. She did not have the knowing of destiny's workings, but perhaps she could nudge its course like pennies on a pendulum to keep its hundredths.

"Friend, wait then until one black of heart and foul of deed comes calling. You shall know them by these words: Payment I have not, but I know all and seek fortune's fate."

"Anything for the miller's daughter—the one who sought a demon and lived."

"Thala, if it pleases."

"Seymond the Weary I be. Well met, my lady Thala."

Old Fellow awaited on the shore rested and munching on the verge. From there they retraced their journey.

"Mice ever gnaw at the roots of enchanted trees. Beset cats upon them and the tree will again bear a miraculous bounty," said she at the Town of the Dying Tree. When the townspeople dug holes and found the trueness of the words, they rewarded Thala with two mules: one laden with the last of their coffer's gold and the other silver.

"A fat toad blocks the workings. Remove it and the well will once again be flush with wine," said she at the Town of the Parched Fountain. When the townspeople set to work and found the toad, they showed their gratitude and gifted a mule packed with fine wine and rubies.

At long last, Thala reached the castle and presented the three golden hairs. The Prince could hardly contain his delight, but the Queen—displeased to see Thala but more pleased over the riches— took the hairs and threw them in a brazier hoping to expose the pauper as a fraud. The hairs did not burn, and the flames made their gold shine as new.

"You prove yourself a thief!" The Queen accused and scowled even as she lifted the rubies and let them run through her fingers.

Thala lifted her chin, smudged with the road and layers of travel grime. "I am Thala, a miller's daughter, righter of broken things, and the One Who Sought a Demon and Lived. No thief am I."

Prince Osric tried to ply his mother with diplomacy. "She has returned and done all that was bidden," said he, but the Queen heard none of it.

"How then did you get such riches if not by robbery?"

"One does not steal what is given freely. Let my family live unburdened and I shall tell you where I found fortune."

"See, my son? Devious and corrupt. She is not for you." The Queen—ever consumed by the lure of all that glittered—considered the offer while she fiddled with the gold and silver. "Done!"

"At the end of the wayroad where the Amaranthine River meets the Farlands you will find a ferry. Stop not for anything and you might find the ferryman there still. He will ask who comes and what payment. Tell him this: Payment I have not, but I know all and seek fortune's fate. Do as I say and all you deserve shall be handed to you."

Thala was escorted out of the castle at once and the Queen set off in haste with her personal guard. But the miller's daughter, righter of broken things, and the One Who Sought a Demon and lived, had not yet finished the quest she had forged with the Prince. She met him at the far gates where they'd talked and there planted one of the precious seeds at the base and whispered this: "Break the chains and let Prince Osric be freed."

The Prince found her there as he had hoped, entreated for her forgiveness, and professed his affections a safe distance from the enchanted boundaries.

"Majesty, I regret my heart does not pine for you and I beg your pardon. I still desire not to marry, Your Highness." For all the politeness, Thala did not curtsy nor lower her head. This boldness only deepened the Prince's admiration and he could not hide his disappointment.

"As my lady wishes."

"I am no lady, Highness."

"A lady you have always been. And might I say, 'tis treason to argue with the Prince."

Thala was gladdened by his smile and encouraged him forward. "I have brought back that which you most yearn for. The way is open."

The Prince stepped through and the roses did not appear. Instead, the ensorcell burst and sprouted as a vine with tiny mauve blooms. So overjoyed was he that Osric forgot all propriety, wept, and embraced Thala. He did not let her go until she quite had to beg for a moment to draw breath.

"What shall you do now?" asked he.

"I have one last wish to make," said she.

Home she and Old Fellow went with an escort, her riches, and blessings from the Prince. Thala's parents were so overjoyed to have her back and plied her with so much affection that they didn't see what she'd brought for a full half turn of an hour. She could not tear herself away from them until she had told her story and days had passed. In the pre-dawn of the third morning, she slipped away to speak to the White River.

"I understand and see you, friend," said she to the waters. Into a hole at the bank where she often sat to listen to the courses and burbles beneath a three-pillared pavilion, she dropped the last seed and whispered: "Break the chains and set the White River free."

A young man with long, white flowing hair, brown mud skin, and pale aquamarine eyes—quite naked to be sure—burst from the depths and gasped a first breath. He laughed, startled himself at the sound, and laughed again.

"What shall I call you?" asked she.

"I have no name," replied he, for he had never been human before.

"When you find it, you'll know."

They were as old friends ought to be in those early days and their affections matured over time. The River was eager to explore, but always returned to the mill (where ensorcell bloomed most profuse) in the summers. He would find Thala traveling the village with Old Fellow and offering her tinkering services—though she had riches enough to never need work and an official title bestowed by King Osric. "If not as my bride, then be as my kin," said he.

One summer in the third year, the River found his name and Thala found her heart for matrimony. They wed at Red's Inn though many questioned the selection of a known robber's den despite the blessings and attendance of His Royal Highness. As of what became of the murderous King, the Queen—quite incensed at his tomfoolery—hired seven rabble to kidnap him and paid a tidy sum for his passage on a ship with the blackest reputation to take him to the farthest port of the foulest city. None have heard from the wretch since.

It is also said that where the Amaranthine River meets the shores of the Farlands, a woman in royal rags ferries back and forth and back and forth without end, and if you pay a man named Seymond the Saved, he will tell you the story of how a queen became a ferryman and how fortune's daughter sought a demon but found herself.

ABOUT THE AUTHOR

Tara lives in Massachusetts with her husband, two children, two old cats, and an incorrigible dog. She has a B.S. degree in Biology from the University of Massachusetts at Dartmouth and teaches Algebra at a local college. Having completed her debut short-story  collection, Tara can be found writing flash fiction on her personal blog and working on her first novel. Her favorite stories to write involve a dose of science fiction, a dash of wit, and a lingering sense of creep.

http://www.facebook.com/taradavisauthor
tdavisauthor@yahoo.com
http://twitter.com/tdavisauthor
#mindfulthings

* * *

In my head words live.
Neurons fire chemical pens.
I dream; stories wake.